THE SEXUAL LIFE OF
AN ISLAMIST IN PARIS

Leïla Marouane

THE SEXUAL LIFE OF AN ISLAMIST IN PARIS

*Translated from the French
by Alison Anderson*

Europa
editions

Europa Editions
116 East 16th Street
New York, N.Y. 10003
www.europaeditions.com
info@europaeditions.com

First Publication 2010 by Europa Editions

Translation by Alison Anderson
Original title: *La vie sexuelle d'un islamiste à Paris*
Translation copyright © 2009 by Europa Editions

Library of Congress Cataloging-in-Publication Data is available
ISBN 978-1-933372-85-3

Marouane, Leïla
The Sexual Life of an Islamist in Paris

Book design by Emanuele Ragnisco
www.mekkanografici.com

Prepress by Plan.ed – Rome

Printed in Canada

CONTENTS

THE SEXUAL LIFE OF
AN ISLAMIST IN PARIS

With thanks to "Mohamed"
for his trust and his outspokenness.

PART ONE
DISSIDENCE

"Before you are someone, you must first be no one."
L'Ombilic des limbes
Antonin Artaud

"Biological racism has given way to cultural racism. It is no longer the color of one's skin or the shape of one's nose that are stigmatized, but a certain manner of being."
Les Damnés de la terre
Frantz Fanon

It came over me all of a sudden, he said. I was at my desk, hardly listening to my client, and I couldn't take my eyes off the dome that was shining like a mirage beyond the bay window. You're in Paris but you're not in Paris. A shadow passing through the city. Morning after morning. Going back to the gray skies of your *banlieue*. Night after night. Paris shines for other people. You're becoming lackluster, there among your family. That's the point you're at, old boy. Strolling by the banquet, not allowed to taste. Existing without an existence.

I'm fed up with this situation, I said again, so distraught that I immediately had to cut short the appointment with my client.

A few minutes later, with the smile of the perfect capitalist plastered on my face, I was seeing my client to the door. I told my assistant I'd be out for a while, and I left the office.

I smoked a cigarette, watched the passers-by, looked at the shop windows, the cars . . . Then I strolled around for a while. Like someone stretching their legs to empty their mind. My mind was boiling over, and my feet refused to advance any further.

I looked at the passersby again, gauging their faces, as if I were looking for something encouraging, and then, brushing aside any thoughts that might interfere with my intention, I ordered my feet to keep going.

A moment later I was outside the real-estate agency that is located a few yards away from the bank where I had just been posted on the rue de Sèvres. I looked through the list of rentals, and then at some of the photos of the interiors, and finally at the price of rents: four digits minimum, enough to take your breath away. But I was ready for anything. I picked out a two-and-a-half-room apartment on the rue Saint-Placide, and went through the door into the agency.

It was of June 26, of the year 2006, the penultimate Friday of the month. As I left the agency, although a stiff breeze was sweeping through the city, I could feel the sweat soaking my shirt.

That same evening, in Saint-Ouen, in the apartment where I'd lived since my tenth birthday—in other words, for thirty whole years—out of sight of my mother and my younger brother I filled out the agency's application form: name, date and place of birth, profession, nationality, and so on. In the square marked "current address," I put my younger sister's address in the 7th arrondissement of Paris, which made me look good to my employers and where, for reasons I will explain below, I was actually receiving all my administrative correspondence.

When I'd finished with the application form, I began to check and sort and classify all the required documents in order: ID, three most recent pay stubs, tax papers . . . Nothing was missing.

Easy peasy Japaneasy, I smiled, scratching my neck with the cap of my ballpoint pen. You are number one, old man, I thought, flattering myself without a trace of irony. Even your mug in the photo doesn't give away a thing about your origins, your skin looks even paler than it is in reality. No cause to be jealous of any white guy. Lucky dog. Your whitening creams and hair straightening sessions on the Avenue Rochechouart have been effective, incontestably. Long live progress . . .

Pleased with my file, which ought to set me up nicely to

make my escape, I started murmuring and humming "Curly locks curly locks wilt thou be mine?" and if anyone had come in on me at that moment, they might have seriously questioned the state of exaltation I was in . . .

I had reached a certain point in my murmurings and hummings when my mother appeared on the threshold to my room. She noticed my ecstatic behavior right away and said, "You look all funny, apple of my eye . . . "

"It's nothing, my mother," I said, recovering my composure.

My usual gloomy and sullen demeanor, that is, the one I've been going around with for a while already, maybe since my father died fifteen years ago. Or maybe since some time after that. Or maybe since always. What do I know. The fact remains that my sullen face meant she'd leave me in peace over dinner, dinner which we ate together, my mother, my brother and myself, night after night. Enough to discourage them from their favorite topic, that is, was I going out with anyone, some girl I might introduce them to, because the ones chosen by my mother did not tend to find grace in my eyes, and my temples were going gray, and my brother's temples would very soon do likewise, although he was already engaged, but was prepared to respect tradition, and was waiting for nothing else, therefore, than for his older brother to get married so that he in turn might be wed.

In short, I donned my usual demeanor and, reassured, my mother said, "Your dinner is getting cold, light of my days, and your brother is getting impatient."

I locked my file away in the drawer where I hid all my administrative documents as well as my poetry manuscripts, and slipped the key into my pocket.

"This obsession of yours with locking things away," said my mother irritably. "As if we were strangers, apple of my eye."

"I'm coming," I said calmly.

I put my ballpoint into my old genuine-leather pencil case, a gift from my late father when I started high school, and I followed my mother out the door.

The next morning, he continued, while my brother and mother were saying the morning prayer, I avoided offering any explanation for my hasty departure, and slipped out the door.

An hour later I left my car in the parking lot at Sèvres-Babylone, in my usual spot. As I was early, I located the nearest brasserie, and sat down on the *terrasse*, well away from the cacophony that regularly accompanied the sun in its estival levitation. A cacophony of luxury languages, that is—English, German, and something that might have been Norwegian or Swiss German—and not a single wog or tar-face in sight. This is standard in neighborhoods frequented by nationals of countries with honorable economic growth and commensurate purchasing power. This is standard in neighborhoods that are deserted in the summer months by those of precarious income, who in any event do not show their faces in sidewalk cafés. This is standard in the neighborhood that will accommodate my days and my joys, I thought with a frisson as I ordered.

I drank my coffee and glanced through my application one last time. Then I checked my watch—only a few minutes left until my appointment. I put a five-euro note on the saucer and, without waiting for change, got to my feet. I looked at my watch again, and headed for the building directly across the street from the brasserie.

I decided against the elevator, and at full speed, without pausing, I climbed all five flights of stairs. On the landing, like a sprinter, I breathed out in short little puffs. When my heartbeat had returned to normal, I admired the double door made of solid wood and wrought iron, then buttoned the first two buttons of my linen jacket and smoothed it carefully. I made sure that my file was still in my leather briefcase, that I hadn't abandoned it there amongst all the high-end tourists, and, on the very stroke of eight A.M., as punctual as a denizen of Switzerland, I rang the bell.

Perfect, I thought, as we toured the apartment. Perfect, I thought over and over, feeling as if I had wandered onto a film set.

Oak parquet flooring all through the apartment. It's been sealed, said the young woman from the agency; walls so high, between nine and twelve feet, that you practically had to twist your neck around to admire the molding on the ceiling; an entrance where I could put a little chest and an armchair; a double living room with fireplace and the original mirrors, alcoves, and moldings—I could picture a leather sofa and armchairs, a modern carpet, a designer lamp, and a little bar decorated to my taste and that of my guests; a dressing room that could easily house a family of gypsies and that would be perfect for my designer clothes; a kitchen of sky-blue earthenware tiles, with a loggia overlooking the courtyard, an American bar the size of a studio, where I could organize my candlelight dinners; a bedroom with the original fireplace and mirror, alcoves and moldings, overlooking a leafy courtyard—I've heard that a blackbird lives in the plane tree, explained my guide, while I determined where the bookshelf would go, along with the desk, facing the window, above the foliage that would inspire poetry to make Antonin Artaud and Octavio Paz weep in unison in their graves, and then of course the bed, maybe a palatial king-size, where I would roll about with creatures to tempt angels and demons alike; a bathroom in tones of green and yellow, two sinks side by side, an oval tub that could easily seat two adults and into which I would plunge each of my future conquests and myself along with them; a separate toilet with a bookshelf that went right to the ceiling, where I would place my collections of *Diplo* and *Politics*, my graphic novels, and the girlie magazines I intended to acquire; and all the closets, wide and deep, and all the copper doorknobs, as old as the mirrors . . . And all of it just like new. Now all I had to do was settle in, according to my dream.

I was admiring the mirror above the fireplace when the young woman's reflection appeared in it. I turned around to look at her. While she was talking about this and that, things to do with the building—the neighbors, most of them owners, aging residents, often absent, particularly in the summer, no children, of course, two apartments on each landing, no one directly opposite, sublime peace and quiet, and the concierge, Madame Lisa, discreet and efficient, who was in her loge from eight to twelve and then again from two to four, every day except Sunday and holidays, and she handed out the mail and so on—my nostrils were suddenly assailed by her delicately spicy perfume, and I began to observe her with the intense interest of a virgin who is only too ready to put his virginity behind him.

Thirty years old, scarcely more, tall, almost my height, in any event much taller than the average Frenchwoman, blonde hair cut short, revealing the harmonious curve of her neck, tight trousers and a discreet but suggestive neckline, shoulders wide and muscular, hips narrow: she gave off something androgynous, almost mannish, and very sexy. But from her eyes, which were blue and heavily made up, there exuded a sort of malevolence—was it scorn? at any rate it was unpleasant—that immediately turned me off.

This is all pink marble, she said, sliding her hand over the mantelpiece. And in perfect condition, she added in her professional tone of voice. While she was urgently advising me to have the chimney swept any time after September, I began to imagine scenes from my future life. Naked as the day I was born, on a plush carpet, there I'd be, warming myself by the fireplace and at the very vaginal source of a blonde or a brunette or a redhead or, why not, all three at the same time, going from one sex to the next, breathing in, drinking my fill from all their secretions, which I imagined to be as sweet as honey, as fragrant as musk. My thighs trembled, a thousand butterflies brushed my skin with their powdery wings, and I went hard. As a rock.

A moment later, as if I had been found out, my ears turned bright red. I discreetly fastened the third button on my jacket and stopped moving. As soon as my gaze alighted on my guide's blue eyes, everything went slack.

I walked over to the wide-open door to the balcony and once again had the impression I was in a film. Would I be the hero, or just a mere extra? My heart began to pound against my ribs, my thorax went tight, and I felt a burning in my guts.

And what if, for some reason or other, they wouldn't rent this little Versailles to me? What if this blonde with her malevolent gaze grew suspicious at the sight of my birthplace and decided to get hold of a copy of my birth certificate, only to come upon the entry, "Name Frenchified, such-and-such a day and month and year"? And thereby discovered my birth name at the bottom of the page? My birth name was that of my father, who was an only son and who had lost both parents in the war—the Second World War, it goes without saying—and of my paternal great-uncle, who had raised my father because he was a *native* at the time, unlike those *compatriots* including one young Camus, Albert by name, my father had not been able to benefit from the status of *war orphan of the Nation.*

The name of my paternal great-uncle who, as I was saying, was also my father's father-in-law, my maternal grandfather, therefore, a man as pious as Bendy,[1] but also as wise as Gandhi.

---

[1] Bin Laden (clarification provided by Mohamed).

In any event, throughout his entire life this man who had raised my father did nothing but good deeds, and would have been utterly incapable of attacking even the meanest of flies that swarmed over us in the summer in Blida, my place of birth, as it happens. Therefore my father, an illiterate worker at Renault who was doomed to die of fatigue and melancholy, was much pleased upon seeing my results at school, and then, further encouraged by my mother, he moved heaven and earth to undertake a naturalization procedure on my behalf. As far as he was concerned, he couldn't care less about nationality; he was neither a doctor or a lawyer, a residence permit sufficed amply for a worker like him. Nor did he undertake the procedure for his eldest daughter, my twin sister, who was a good student on top of it but still too much of a flirt, and no one viewed her future in this debauched country in a favorable light; therefore her life as a wife and mother would be among her family, in our town, in our country, in Blida, as advocated by my mother. And my father approved. My father, who, despite my timid nod to the employee of the courts, had firmly opposed my name change. Ben Mokhtar we were born, Ben Mokhtar we shall die, he exulted as we left the courthouse, calling me his *Doctor*, okay so now I was a Frenchman, but I was still Mohamed Ben Mokhtar, son and grandson of Ben Mokhtar. Aren't you, my son?

Yes, my father, I promised, with all the gravity of my sixteen years.

B ut, said he, just before I finished my studies at HEC, the famous business school, with the support of Martine—the lady in whose care, upon our arrival on French soil and while waiting to find decent accommodation, my twin sister and I had been placed—I wrote to the state prosecutor.

A letter where I expressed the wish to Frenchify my name. In the blink of an eye my name was Frenchified. It goes without saying that my family, who are real sticklers for principles, were totally ignorant of my new name—which explains the address lent to me by my sister who had become my friend and accomplice shortly after her ostracism from the tribe for having consorted with a *roumi* who stubbornly refused to convert to our religion.

Whatever the case may be, with my new identity, my hair straightened, and my skin whitened, I did not suffer from any discrimination due to my origins. The path before me was wide open. And the doors. And arms. Please, Monsieur Tocquard, come this way. You're very welcome, Monsieur Basile Tocquard, just step that way . . .

The name might raise a smile, it's true, but it is more believable, less suspicious, than a Jean Dupont or a Paul Duchemin, or even the Charles Martel suggested by the employee at the courthouse, who was dismayed by a last name that would surely be very difficult to live with, so she said, and who proceeded to inform me that it might be rejected by the authorities. That

I must have substantial grounds . . . Thus, I invented a child-hood friend, no longer with us, whose name had been that very one, Madame, Monsieur. Etc.

Later, when I was settled in that place where wolves howl and men are silent, I wondered whether there was not some-thing premonitory about my choice[1]—or was it not simply that I wanted to punish myself for betraying my grandfather, my father, and all the present-day and future descendants of the Ben Mokhtar clan?

Whether it is a betrayal or not, if my brother, who is ten years younger than I am and who was born French, if he, a research manager with a degree from a good school, had put aside his pride, and gotten rid of his little beard, and smeared his skin with whitening cream, and straightened his little curls, and written to the state prosecutor, he would not be reduced today to rotting like a *meskine* between his mother's walls and those of the neighborhood mosque.

As for me, very early on I abandoned my pride. However, at the time when I began my physical and patronymic meta-morphosis, my piety was on a par with that of my brother, and my knowledge of Islam far surpassed his own.

I was the good Muslim, the kind of Islamist—nowadays we would say "fundamentalist" or "terrorist"—who was respected and solicited for advice by the entire neighborhood. To such an extent that I was called on to lead prayers, or recite a ser-mon, or give my opinion on questions from simple to compli-cated. What was to be done if a child inadvertently ate pork at the school cafeteria? Should one allow one's wife to be exam-ined by a male physician? Could one accept a job in a bar? Or

[1] One should note that there is in the name Basile the French word for asylum, "*asile*"; as for the eloquence of Tocquard, what better homonym for our word for loser, ugly, useless . . . (Mohamed).

a butcher's shop? Should one allow one's daughter to remove her headscarf at school, hoping that the angel who keeps tabs on such misdeeds won't take them into account?

I confess that from time to time I was forgetful of my late grandfather's tolerance—he was a Sufi who paid no heed to those who threatened him with anathema, in the heart of Blida, a conservative and fanatical town if ever there was one, and who had removed his daughters' veils, including that of my mother, and sent them to school, and, invoking *lakum dinukum wa-li dini*,[2] he allowed his nephew, my father, to seek his sustenance in an ungodly land—and I was as rigid as a pontiff, condemning my fellows to unemployment and placing young girls in inextricable dilemmas . . .

I was, thus, the perfect Muslim but, unlike my brother, I began an intimate acquaintance with the administration the moment I arrived in France in the mid-1970s, when I was not yet ten years old, and my brother was only barely conceived.

I nurtured this acquaintance at my father's request and in his company: not only did I act as public scribe for him, filling out his applications and checking the answers in the right place, but I was also his interpreter, in the event that a word or a phrase might slip past him, and, with the exception of remarks which might make the most implacable among us fly off the handle, everything slipped past my old man, who never flew off the handle and remained silent even regarding the deterioration of his physical and psychological health.

As soon as my father was of age, and long before the independence of his country, with the shirt on his back and a laborer's card in his pocket, he came to sweat blood and tears for the edification of France, living hand to mouth, here and there, in seedy hotels and migrant workers' barracks, waiting until 1965,

---

[2] Verse indicating that religions may mingle without harm to each other (Mohamed). ("Unto you your religion and unto me my religion," Al-Kafirun 6.)

when he was thirty-two, to marry his very young cousin, my mother, a woman of learning to be sure, but thin and dark, impossible therefore to marry off to anyone other than this illiterate orphan who, for nine whole years, had honored her with his paid leave, while he waited for the day when he would be rich—not as rich as Croesus, but with a few savings nonetheless—and could return to his little family for good.

His savings did not accumulate, or at least not in sufficient amounts for him to pack his trunk, but there did come a presidential decree on family reunification, so the little family in question, now enriched by two children, my twin and myself, came to join him in the land where, even today, I get the impression that I can smell emanations of his sweat.

It is while we were scouring those administrative offices, as I was saying—town halls and police precincts, low-income-housing agencies and family allowance boards, feeling ashamed of my father and his Arabic name, his complexion and his curls, the poverty of his vocabulary and the way he would muffle his steps and his voice—that my pride forced me to up the stakes.

However much it might cost me, willy-nilly, on the sly or in broad daylight, as a worker or as an astronaut, I would lighten my skin, I would straighten my hair, and, naturally, I would swap my name for anything else, provided it had nothing Arabic-sounding about it: this became my refrain, played whenever my father uttered phrases in his pidgin French.

I had initially thought of names such as Sami Massi or Elias Sansal, easy to pronounce, somewhat ambiguous, or so I thought; they would not be off-putting and consequently would not completely alter my identity.

It was only at the high school—which was, however, a private establishment in a posh neighborhood, between Ternes and Wagram, where my mother, wagering on my intellectual gifts, bleeding herself dry on my behalf, and encouraged by

Martine, had decided to enroll me—that I realized that Mohamed, Sami, or Elias: it's all one and the same. Only a *completely* French name, with nothing suspicious about it, would allow me to blend into the mass of white people.

And that is how Basile Tocquard[3] was born. And when I graduated from business school, the headhunters, along with employers at job interviews, were none the wiser.

Would things be the same with this real-estate agency in the 6th arrondissement? I wondered, as I stared at the pink marble fireplace. Hello? Monsieur Mo-ha-med Ben-mok-tar? Uh, Tocquard? The Sèvres agency, here . . . We are sorry to inform you . . .

How, in the name of a roof, would I survive the fireplace? the oval bathtub? the oak parquet flooring? the desk overlooking the foliage? the poems I would not write? the women I would not enjoy?

How would I ever get over the frustration?

I could pack it all in and enroll in one of Bin Laden's multinationals, for example—given my age and my degrees, they'd hire me on the spot. I might even be given the honor of slashing the skies of Manhattan. *Who knows?*

And if the genes of my well-behaved forebears took precedence, in other words, if I lacked the *balls* to carry out this sort of endeavor, I could seek asylum in the land of my parents, and wed the daughter of the mayor of the seaside town north of Blida, the very young and very beautiful girl that my mother, ignoring my scowl, had just set her heart on.

My sweet young thing would give me a few boys—ten, let's say. Ten sturdy and intelligent boys, like their father, who would teach them, with tact and brilliance, how to spit on France and all the West without distinction.

[3] Inspired by the cruelty of my schoolmates (Mohamed).

Honestly, who do they think they are, those white folk? holding our ancestors in contempt and scorn, denigrating their origins and their names? And they have the nerve to claim they brought well-being[4] to the land of our ancestors, while even today, in 2007, they continue to deny us access to their posh neighborhoods, their prestigious jobs, their nightclubs. As if we were still natives, the savages in their colonies.

[4] The official position taken following the introduction of a law on February 23, 2005, which was finally repealed by Jacques Chirac. Thank you Monsieur le Président (Mohamed). (Among other things, the law enjoined high-school teachers to teach the "positive values" of colonialism to their students. T.N.)

After visiting the apartment, he continued, we went back to the agency. The young woman, courteous and professional, just as she would be with anyone of her own blood, offered me a seat, and this made me forget my inner tirade and my cock-and-bull plans.

Sitting down behind the desk, in the very spot where, the evening before, her boss had welcomed me, she picked up my file and said, "I'll take a look at your file. But, Monsieur . . . "

"Tocquard. Basile Tocquard."

"I should warn you, Monsieur Tocquard, that we have had other applicants for this apartment," she said, all in one breath, without batting an eyelid.

"Fine," I said, making a mental evaluation of the contents of my file and, above all, my emoluments—not a mere four digits, proof enough of a worthy school and an honorable trajectory, but five.

Her eyebrow arched, feigning such concentration that you might have thought she was immersed in a dissertation on genetics, the young woman began to consult my file, lingering over the pay stubs and the tax return.

A few moments later, she said, "You have an excellent file, Monsieur Tocquard."

"Good," I said, with a faint smile.

"I'm going to make a photocopy and fax it over to the

owner," she said, getting to her feet. "He's the one who'll get back to you. In general he responds fairly quickly."

"Good," I said, watching her operate the machines, and eyeing her butt on the sly, as flat and manly as her shoulders, but nonetheless sexy and disturbing.

When she had finished photocopying and faxing my file, she sat back down and handed it to me.

"Once the owner has called you, you will come back to see me for the inventory of fixtures and to sign the lease," she said. "And, given your file, he may offer you a six-year lease instead of a three-year one. In either case, we'll start the lease from August 1. But you'll have your keys before that. That way you can move in at your own pace," she continued, discreetly fluttering her eyelashes.

All aquiver and certain of being in possession of the place of my dreams, I once again smiled faintly, although the young woman did not notice, busy as she now was tapping away on a calculator. She jotted endless strings of figures down on a sheet of paper that was, I could see, top quality letterhead. Astronomical sums. It goes without saying. But, once again, I was ready for anything. My freedom had no price, and I had ample means to live the way I intended to live from now on. In splendor and depravity, I thought, eyeing the young woman's lightly suntanned bosom.

"You will need to prepare a check corresponding to each of the amounts I've designated," she said, handing me the fine sheet of paper. "Two months deposit and the rent for the current month, to the order of the owner, and our fees, to the order of the agency. Monsieur Galland, the owner, would prefer a bank transfer, and naturally, don't forget to insure the apartment and send us a copy of the policy. It's required by law."

"Not a problem," I said, careful with the way I enunciated this first sentence, its negation, avoiding any inflection that might reveal my life in the slum belt, that might betray my true-false address in the 7th arrondissement, that might ruin my excellent application . . .

"Insurance for a banker . . . " she said, an imperceptible glimmer suddenly altering the chill in her eyes.

Convinced that she would cancel the other visits, I grabbed the sheet of paper. I slipped it carefully among the other documents in my file, and was getting ready to stand up when, her elbows on the table, her cheeks supported by her carefully groomed hands, her blue eyes staring not into my eyes but at my forehead, she added, "Your file really is very good, Monsieur Tocquard."

"Good," I said, observing her hands, then her rings, which adorned not her ring fingers but the middle ones.

"Nevertheless, I am obliged to keep the other appointments."

I swallowed, transfixed, and she noticed.

"They're scheduled for next week," she continued, with a pout to express her regret.

"Fine, fine," I said.

Without swallowing.

Despite my flawless file, my substitute name, and my true-false address, this white woman is no fool, far from it, and she's uncovered my true origins, I thought, wiping my hand over my left temple, where there were still a few tight curls that resisted the expert fingers of my coiffeur and where this woman who henceforth held in her hands the destiny of a liberated, affluent man, had often directed her gaze, first in the reflection of the mirror above the fireplace, and then here, at the agency, when she sat back down at her boss's desk.

"In any event, the final decision is the owner's," she said.

"Fine," I said, venturing a smile.

A smile that she recorded by broadening her own, her perfect teeth illuminating the blue of her eyes. Then she lifted a hand and reached for her business card, which she handed to me with the utmost grace.

"You can reach me at all times, here at the agency, or on my cell phone," she said, rolling each syllable.

I read her name and said, "Thank you, Madame Agnès Papinot."

"Mademoiselle," she said.

"Forgive me," I said.

"No harm done," she said, without dropping her smile.

And I said nothing more. Nor did she, but given this sudden amicability, it went without saying that she wished to start up a conversation, just to keep me there a bit longer, just to attain some objective.

Sure of her charm, or so I believed at first, this white woman with her malevolent gaze, who scorned my race and my little curls but revered my pay stubs and my Hugo Boss jacket, aspired to only one thing—to tie the knot, around my neck.

First we'd live together, in sin and in the apartment on the rue Saint-Placide—which she would furnish according to *our* taste—little dinner parties with friends, flicks on Saturday, Sunday lunch at parents'—hers, it goes without saying—regular vacation, summer and winter, on the Nile or in Crete, Chamonix, or Switzerland, *warum nicht meine Liebe*, shopping with the credit card belonging to yours truly . . .

And then, once the probity of the pigeon—myself, as it happens—has been confirmed, the wedding bands will be chosen, the time for a little trip to the Town Hall will come, then the ceremony at the same church where her Mom and Dad said "I do," and then finally it will be time to move into a house, with the perspective of inflating the local demographics; in other words there will be three of us, or four, maybe even five, and they'll be called Gustave or Auguste, Clémence or Camille. That too goes without saying.

And who gives a damn about the genitor's tight little curls, anyway? Doesn't he have a degree from HEC? or so they would whisper, her mother and father, her uncle and aunt, her godmother and godfather . . .

I wasn't born yesterday, I knew the refrain.

But maybe, I thought, conscious of her status as a little real-estate agent, maybe she knew that this could never be. In our day and age, to see one's wishes fulfilled, it was not enough to have a nice ass, or exceptional irises, or skill in fluttering one's eyelashes. Doctors no longer married their nurses, nor did bankers marry secretaries or real-estate agents. I would gladly fuck her, and not once but twice, and then send her packing back to her little studio (probably in the suburbs), where she would continue to vegetate, moping in front of American TV series, envying the model spouses, eating an apple and some low-cal cereal for dinner, squandering her meager income at the gym and in beauty salons and low-end boutiques, without even the hope of seducing someone like Nawar, that Lebanese guy, your neighbor, a former client of the rue Saint-Denis, who's become a friend of sorts, whom I ran into in the 6th arrondissement, a good-looking guy, but dark skinned with frizzy hair as visible as the nose on your face, who recently married an aging, anorexic blonde who abhors Arabs but who, given the profession of her young husband—struggling musician, but an artist all the same—considers that *with him it's not the same*, or so he would tell me, on occasion, during our intimate little exchanges in my office.

As for me, sweetheart, I'm neither a gigolo nor a struggling artist, and as for white women—blondes, brunettes, redheads, with eyes of blue, green, gray, violet, or brown, with a kindly gaze thrown in as a bonus, whose aims are quite the opposite of your own, in other words, women who are liberated from conventions, fans of *Sex and the City*—I'll find them. If need be, I'll go all the way to the Revolutionary Communist League to find them.

And as if reading my thoughts, with that malevolent spark

in her eye, the witch said, "The other visits are scheduled for next Wednesday and Thursday."

"Fine," I said, getting to my feet.

She did the same, and walked around the desk to stand facing me. Opening her arms slightly to either side, she said, "And if ever your application doesn't go through, Monsieur Tocquard, above all, please don't hesitate to call me . . . "

As if magnetized, my gaze caught on her neckline. She noticed, and her eyes emanated that vanity which she wore as well as her blue eyes, her blondeness, her neckline, her perfume, her tight trousers, her knowingly manicured hands, and her unequivocal origins.

"Any time," she added.

Then, without any segue, she began talking about her work, told me that she was only temporary there, that other agencies, not located in the 6th arrondissement, also made use of her services, and that she would be sure to find me the very best place: "An apartment in the 18th or 20th arrondissement would be *perfect* for you, Monsieur Tocquard.

"That said," she concluded, "I would advise you to buy rather than rent."

At last I grasped the businesswoman's sudden interest in me: a substantial commission, perhaps even the offer of a permanent position, I thought, and I was about to retort that only this apartment interested me when I changed my tack. Feigning contentment—above all, she must not be allowed to sabotage my plans—I said, "I hadn't thought about it, but it's a good idea."

"Fine," she exulted, walking with me to the door.

"Fine," I repeated, without exulting, imagining that this precariously employed real-estate agent would, no sooner had she gotten rid of me, rush to the telephone, dial Monsieur Galland's number, and inform him that *Monsieur Basile Tocquard has withdrawn his application . . .*

"Goodbye, Monsieur Tocquard," she said, holding out her hand for my handshake.

Thinking of the supporting role I had just played in this little Versailles drama and rejecting it, I was about to invite her to lunch, to the Petit Lutétia, why not, the chic restaurant on the other side of the rue de Sèvres, opposite the real-estate agency—a good meal and a little chitchat ought to convince her to cancel the other visits—but I let go of her hand and turned on my heels, my throat tight, my bowels on fire.

And then, he said, I went through hell. For an entire week I scarcely ate a thing; I smoked one cigarette after another, and got annoyed at the drop of a hat. The tablets of Lexomil I swallowed without counting didn't fix a thing. My mother attributed my sudden (very) bad mood to a romantic disappointment—You can tell your mother everything, light of my days, she ventured, in between the *chorba* and the bell pepper salad, my favorite dishes, and which stayed desperately uneaten on my plate. Or could it have been the excess of testosterone that a man owes it to himself to evacuate—And the mayor's daughter, you know . . . she ventured again, directing subtle winks at my brother, who concluded that it was the stress of working in Paris that was behind my nervous collapse, and she suggested I request a transfer.

"You were better off in Saint-Denis," he said, squinting at me, raising his voice.

"I'm fine in Paris," I insisted, pushing back my plate.

At which point my mother interrupted her meal and rushed off to fix me some hot milk with honey. And my brother, remembering who was the eldest in the house, and powerless in any event in the face of so much irascibility, eventually lowered his gaze and his voice.

After I had smoked a few cigarettes in my car—I had not been smoking for long, and never did so at home—I sat alone as long as I could in the kitchen, brooding, resigning myself to the idea that I would continue to spend my life tied to my mother's apron strings, surrendering, submitting to the destiny that had been allotted me.

The sacrifice of Isaac, as my colleague Gad would say.

The sacrifice of Ishmael, as my cousin, and friend, Driss would say.

A pointless life, I mumbled, going to my bedroom.

To fall asleep, overwhelmed by my brother's wheezing—he who, strong in his faith, confiding his failures and sorrows to his Creator, was sleeping like a dormouse—I had to take double the usual dose of Stilnox, along with the other medication I'd been prescribed following my father's death. A treatment I was following, suffice to say, unbeknownst to my family. Because a man, a real man, *where we come from*, in my family, in any case, shouldn't need subterfuges, and certainly shouldn't be consulting those who prescribe them.

At work, despite the office's *cool, Zen* atmosphere, as my closest colleagues called it, the least little thing exasperated me. I cancelled important appointments, locked myself in my office, and gave the order that I was not to be disturbed under any circumstance—except if, and only if, a certain Monsieur Galland were to call—and I sat before the computer screen scrolling through the apartments for rent on the Internet, but my heart wasn't in it. Only the nest on the rue Saint-Placide found favor in my eyes. It was there or nowhere, I thought. And what if I invited Mademoiselle Agnès Papinot for lunch? Perhaps then she would *omit* faxing my rivals' files to the owner, and she would call him back to revoke my purported withdrawal. That way I would end up as the only applicant for the little Versailles.

I stared at her business card, sat for a long while deciphering the telephone numbers, land line and cellular, and her e-mail address. There was no postal address. My assumptions were therefore correct, she lived in the slum belt, and avoided putting her address on her card, a tactic I was only too familiar with after having resorted to it myself, before I was reconciled with my sister, the disowned one. Meditating on the fate of poor Mademoiselle Papinot, I eventually abandoned the idea of contacting her. It was pointless to stoop that low. And if things did not turn out the way I hoped, if I did not obtain the object of my desires, that little nest that obsessed me, well, I would just have to find a way to get the necessary credit, and I would acquire the apartment of my dreams, somewhere between the rue du Cherche-Midi and the rue de Sèvres. And fate, without the intervention of that blonde with her malevolent gaze, would continue in its work.

So be it, I thought, to console myself, putting away her business card.

And so it was.

As I was staring relentlessly at the dome of the Invalides, scarcely listening to the client who was very worried about his investments on the stock exchange, my assistant put through a call from Monsieur Galland.

My aorta was pounding fit to burst, and I excused myself to my client as I pressed the receiver right up against my ear. A few seconds later, lulled by the voice of my new (and very first) landlord, I was bathed in a rosy light and my pulse was beating almost in slow motion. As I put the phone down, I felt like kissing my client on both cheeks.

After my client's departure—and I did not kiss him on his cheeks, nor anywhere else for that matter—I called the real-estate agency. Mademoiselle Agnès Papinot, who had already been informed of the "good news," asked me if I could come by within the hour because, she explained, her mandate at the Sèvres agency would terminate in a few days, around the 13th of July, and she had to settle everything before her departure.

As I put down the receiver, a sudden warmth suffused the office. As if the devil himself, lurking somewhere on the premises, was blowing this heat from all his nostrils.

I loosened my tie, took off my jacket, and stood up. Then, as I was double-checking the air conditioning, which was in perfect working order, I was racked by abdominal spasms so violent that I was forced to bend over—and the furniture in the room began to reel, and the floor beneath my feet to sway . . .

Breathless, struggling against dizziness, I managed to stand up straight. I pressed my back against the wall, and waited for the malaise to pass. A few moments later, the temperature was back to normal and the spasms stopped.

I sat back down, wiped my face, and took a big swallow of water. I cracked my knuckles and then, taking a deep breath, with a rotation of my head I cracked the vertebrae in my neck.

Breathing calmly, I then dug out the sheet of fine letterhead. Diligent as a young schoolboy, I filled out and signed all the checks. When I had finished, I put my checkbook away in the leather briefcase worthy of the financier that I am, and I called my assistant and asked her to draw up a residential insurance policy in my name, at the following address and for so-and-so many square meters . . . If you please, Madame Seguin. Fearful of the evil eye, I hung up before she had the time to proffer anything remotely resembling congratulations.

I put on my jacket and adjusted my tie, but instead of going out, I just stood there looking at the dome of the Invalides. No longer shining like a mirage, but well and truly like the real monument, all gold and arches embellishing my horizon. He's one of us! You're one of them. I'm one of you.

Pleasantly flabbergasted, ready to confront the lovely Agnès Papinot, I finally left my office. On the way, gracing my assistant with a smile, I informed her that I was stepping out, and would probably be absent all afternoon.

My voice, cheerful at last, gave her such pleasure that no less than twice she wished me "An excellent weekend, Monsieur Tocquard." Then, "A lovely summer," reminding me that she was leaving on vacation, that she'd arranged everything; an intern, whom she'd handpicked, would replace her. I was about to ask her if the intern was pretty, then thought better of it.

Mademoiselle Agnès Papinot, he said, was wearing an outfit that clashed with her manly allure, but in no way impinged upon the sensuality of that allure. A skirt above the knee, and a transparent slip rimmed with sequins, in fashion that summer. And not the slightest trace of a bra: her round, firm breasts quivered like young pigeons ready to take flight.

While I avoided staring cross-eyed at her bust, she suggested, given that I was already familiar with the apartment, and knew that I liked it, and in order to save time, that I sign the lease before dealing with the inventory of fixtures. I informed her that the insurance was already pending, and I handed her the checks, then initialed and signed the two copies of the lease. In a very professional tone of voice, she congratulated me and we went over to the rue Saint-Placide.

While she was noting down the condition of the paint, the plumbing, the door and window frames, and so on, I took a moment to examine the entire space of *my* apartment, assuring myself that my first impression had been correct. And it was, incontestably; and incontestably I was madly in love with my abode. My superb magnificent divine nest. Where the most beautiful little birds would, thanks to my ministrations, be

cosseted
cherished
drunk

eaten
nibbled
turned this way and that
in every direction
from every angle
in every posture
licit or illicit
divine or diabolical
I was lifting the blower of the fireplace when Mademoiselle Agnès Papinot, whom I'd almost forgotten, extricated me from my heated deliberation.

"Please don't forget to have it swept," she said.

"Who?" I went, startled.

"The chimney, Monsieur Tocquard."

"Of course, Mademoiselle Papinot," I said, in a voice where I (deliberately) allowed a little allusion to filter through.

An allusion that Mademoiselle Papinot picked up on, but deliberately ignored.

"And please don't forget the bank transfer. Here is Monsieur Galland's IBAN number," she said, handing me an envelope.

"I'll see to it," I said, seizing the envelope.

"Good, then all that's left to do is to approve and sign the inventory of fixtures," she said.

"Fine," I said, struggling against an almost irrepressible desire to fondle her breasts.

"And if you ever are in the mood to buy . . . " she said, in a voice that was so soft, lascivious, her breasts quivering, so close at hand . . .

And what if she were, in the end, on the point of offering herself to me? And what if I were to take her? Here. Now. Right away. Thus, sooner than expected, I would put an end to my chastity. That way, sooner than expected. To explore a woman. Her labyrinthine secrets. Clefts and slits. Whiffs. Secretions and sweat. And Mademoiselle Papinot, manly and sexy, had what it took to placate my cock, which was overheating and overhardening.

A split-second later, thinking back over the week from hell that I had just endured thanks to her, I felt a grudge as big as a dromedary overwhelm me, and my desire to give her a tumble on the varnished parquet floor rapidly receded.

"I have no intention of buying," I said in a neutral voice.

"For the time being," she said, removing a set of keys from her handbag and placing them on the mantelpiece. "But if you change your mind—because it's a pity to pay rent when you have the means to invest—please don't hesitate to call me," she added, tenacious, her voice even softer and more lascivious than before.

"We'll see," I said, struggling against a new and violent erection.

"Well, I think that's everything," she said, miming her departure.

"Yes, I think so," I said, without following her to the door, congratulating myself as I watched her turn on her heels, the way I had turned, a week earlier, my throat tight, my bowels on fire.

But when the door clicked shut, Mademoiselle Papinot's breasts assailed my mind, causing me to regret this missed opportunity to possess them, and to reproach myself for my pathological spite, and to rebuke myself for my incurable paranoia, and with my cock as hard as a rock I hastened to the toilet.

A few minutes later, relieved, I went back into town, and devoted the rest of the afternoon to my shopping. Darty, for household appliances; Habitat, for furniture.

Once I had placed my orders, he said, and had returned to my new *quartier*—I could have pinched myself—I indulged in a few other purchases: a red lamp, factory style and exorbitantly priced at the Conran Shop, on the rue de Babylone, and a coffee maker from the Nespresso boutique on the rue du Bac.

The salesgirl—a pearl of the sort perfectly fashioned to splash around in my oval bathtub—gazed on, duly impressed and jovial as I bought myself four hundred boxes of coffee capsules, from the strongest to the lightest.

I was about to buy half a dozen of the lovely Italian cups, but then I said, "Two cups, please," to indicate that I was neither a head of household nor was I shacked up in any manner, but that I was indeed a bachelor—free, quick, and ready for anything. And besides, that naughty girl, as she reached for my American Express, she gave a furtive glance at my ring finger. Devoid of any wedding ring. That goes without saying. Then she smiled and emoted a friendliness that exceeded the bounds of commerce. I could be sure that the next time I visited the shop she would gladly accept the business card I would discreetly slip her way. Moreover, I would be needing some business cards, with my private address and telephone number. And, naturally, my Gallicized name.

What I would like to emphasize here is the fact that I only had eyes—and desire—for white women, regular users of the pill and the condom, free in their bodies and their minds, women who consciously, with joy and good humor, without scruples or qualms, are headed for lifelong celibacy, unlike Mademoiselle Papinot, manicuring her lovely hands, preserving the ring finger for a wedding band, unlike the young virgins in my suburb, with their obvious virgin-up-to-my-neck, chaste-until-marriage mannerisms.

In any event, even with her consent, I had no intention of defiling a Muslim girl: there would be no taste in it, or at best there would be the insipidity inspired by the *bismillah* without which any act, sexual or otherwise, is illicit.

Thus far had I progressed with the cogitations, analyses, and conclusions of a man henceforth equipped with a cock that was, if not ungodly, at least secular, when I left the shop, titillated by the salesgirl's charm.

Burdened with my luxury parcels, I used my cell phone to call Telecom and order the installation of a landline, headed straight then branched off through the streets of my *quartier*, and found myself on the boulevard Raspail. Near the Hôtel Lutétia, somewhat lost, I rushed across a sort of square that smelled of piss and spilt wine.

On the corner of the boulevard and of the rue du Cherche-Midi I caught my breath and stopped outside a store selling Oriental rugs. Two or three kilims, some cushions, a lamp with multi-colored facets, amphoras, a water pipe: in short, a little oriental salon in a corner of my living room, opposite the fireplace, would not be an excessive luxury. And if my mother, who never left Saint-Ouen, did happen to pay a visit, a place where she could unroll her prayer mat would reassure her on the fate of her son. Oh light of his mother's days, still faithful to his origins and his upbringing. My mother, perpetually clinging. My mother, sticky as a *makrout*. My mother, sticking to her son. However, just as in the old days, when the women in the Kasbah never ventured into the European quarters, my mother never came to the center of Paris—even on those rare occasions when she did leave our suburb, Barbès and the surrounding area remained her limit.

Whatever the case may be, however filled with pity for my progenitor I might be, however aware of her sacrifices, of how she had aged before her time, of her unhealthy thinness, her frustrations, her wasted life, I was far too happy to wallow in any sort of resentment toward my family, and my natural indulgence regained the upper hand. I promised myself I would arrange that space in case my mother, or at any rate my brother, or my sister Ourida, the youngest of the three sisters, the pious, blessed one, along with her convert of a husband, Alain also known as Ali, decided to come for a visit.

I headed up the rue du Cherche-Midi, and toward the top found my own street. My street. In the very heart of Paris. In the most beautiful neighborhood on the planet. And then my building. From the Haussmann era, lofty, freestone . . . But that wasn't all: a gentleman, a man of letters, said the plaque, by the name of Huysmans, born in Paris in 1848, had breathed his last here on May 12, 1907. Thus. In a few decades. Perhaps. My name would be. Carved. In the same place. Born in Blida. In 1966. Wow. Ouch. There is no sure concomitance that is not accompanied by a coincidence, cogitated Bachelard. So I declaimed, punching in the entry code.

Crossing the threshold of my building, I must have looked as happy as a clam, for the woman I passed on the way in, no doubt a neighbor, a sixty-something lady who didn't look like the sort to brighten up easily, gave me a brilliant smile, infected by my euphoria.

Like a cat marking its territory, I spread my parcels all over the place—the lamp on the mantelpiece, the coffee capsules in the cupboard, and the luxury machine on the sink, where I promptly unpacked it. I read the instruction manual and got ready to use it. I rinsed out one of the two cups and made myself a coffee, which I drank standing up, smoking a cigarette and dreaming of my future encounters. Women left and right, wham bam thank you ma'am. Advocates of relations without consequence or change of heart. No lifetime commitments. No procreation.

What purpose would it serve to alienate myself with a woman? I asked, over and over. Or to procreate? What good would a wife do me? What would be the point of having any progeny? Only to sacrifice the career as a poet that awaited me? Worse, even. Only to pile on worries and die alone in a hospital bed. The way my father died. In that hospital, in Blida. Alone, from cirrhosis of the liver.

A few years before he died, he continued, my father took advantage of his early retirement, or so we thought, to go two or three times a year to Blida.

The family home had been divided up among my grandfather's heirs—according to the sharia which was still in force in the land of Algeria, my mother, as a woman, had only inherited a tiny part of it, which she then relinquished to her numerous brothers in exchange for a room that we could use during the summer; as for my father, once again according to the sharia, because he was adopted he had not inherited a thing, and so he stayed here and there, in a hotel, or at the baths.

My mother protested vigorously—the plane ticket was costly, as were the hotels and the baths, not to mention the taverns where he took his meals; my father countered by defending the importance of his trips, emphasizing that he now had a civil servant on his side and that finally, soon, he would be able to acquire the property where he would build a house for us, for my mother, above all, who gave him no peace, constantly harping on about her nostalgia for the land whence she had been torn and where, in the end, my father breathed his last, at the age of fifty-nine, in the spring of the year 1992, the day after I turned twenty-six, the day before my final exam.

My mother, as was fitting, wanted to support me "during this important trial," so there was no question of her, the wife, or of me, the eldest son, going to the side of the dying man. Or even of burying him. Naturally my twin sister, who had finally gone back to Blida and gotten married three years before our father died, could have been at his bedside. But the husband we had chosen for her, for whatever reasons of his own, was not one of those who allows their legitimate spouse out of the house. And women, because they are so emotional, are excluded from funerals, regardless of their age or relationship to the deceased.

Thus, my father breathed his last alone, as if he had never had any family, although the other patients in his ward were there for him all the same, and are thought to have moistened his lips and made sure he recited his *shahada* in time, or so we were informed later by one of my maternal uncles, who had arranged the funeral.

It was also somewhat later, in the autumn following his death, when I went to the factory to take care of some administrative formalities, that I learned that my father drank, and that his premature retirement was actually sick leave, for a long illness. He could not sit up straight in front of the machine, your *old man*, said one of his old friends and coworkers. He had constant hallucinations . . .

No one had a clue at the time that my father was drinking, certainly not my mother, busy as she was raising her two sons—cooking up little dinners for them, dressing them like nabobs, looking for wives for them—and educating her three daughters—keeping close watch on their honor, repatriating the eldest, disowning the second, blessing the youngest—and today I feel remorse that I never saw how my father was suffering, that I never suspected how sick he was, and I'm still amazed at how well he hid it from everyone—saying his prayers without flinching, both at home and at the mosque, obeying without grumbling the demands of his wife, my mother, an educated female, haughty and domineering in her own domain, to whom I have not breathed a word about these revelations which, for days and nights thereafter, obsessed me to the point of insomnia and sent me straight to the door of my psychiatrist.

Resolved to take control of my life as I saw fit, he continued, with neither god nor master, neither wife nor child, I reiterated with sudden jubilation, I finished drinking my coffee and rinsed out my cup. A moment later I was pacing back and forth in the apartment, my mind transfixed, unsure of how to divest myself of this anxiety that clung so stubbornly.

I rummaged in my pockets in search of some Lexomil and then, remembering my determination to be done with these drugs, I gave up. In the bedroom by the wide open window, I fixed my gaze upon the plane tree in the courtyard and, ignorant of the fact that blackbirds only sing at dusk, something Mademoiselle Papinot had not mentioned, I pricked up my ears.

Somewhat disappointed, on the verge of being angry, I went back into the living room and paced up and down. And as if to remind myself of my newfound reality, I opened my personal organizer and began to double-check the date and time when my purchases would be delivered.

Washing machine, dishwasher, fridge, freezer, gas stove, microwave, vacuum cleaner: this coming Thursday, between nine and noon. I would ask the concierge to take care of the delivery men. Because I have a concierge, I murmured. A concierge who, acting as a private post office, will be slipping my mail to me under the door. Is that not royal?

As for the bed, wardrobe, sofa, armchairs, table and chairs, desk, bookshelf, bedding, curtains, tablecloths, napkins, plates, frying pans and casseroles, and sundry wine, champagne, water and whisky glasses, along with only the finest dinnerware: they would be delivered on Monday, my day of rest. I would not forget, when clearing out of Saint-Ouen, walking out on my family, to take my old sleeping bag for Sunday night.

I had deliberately avoided buying a television, and I had left absolutely nothing to chance. A small fortune had been spent. If I'd gone to Leroy-Merlin, I would have spent less than half the amount. But that whole galaxy evoked the third world to me, as I knew it, or some Eastern European country in the thick of the Cold War, and it was utterly off-putting. How many times had I taken my mother there? How many times had we gone up and down the kitchenware aisles like two raving lunatics looking for the cheapest thing available? How many times had my mother thrown her heart into the purchase of a remnant of linoleum—hideous, but could you beat the price? How many times had she ordered me to run after a salesman in the wall-to-wall carpeting department? That's right, me, one of the most sought-after financiers of all the banks in all the realm.

And the racket. And the line at the checkout. And the smells of sweat and cheap perfume and aftershave . . . I leave the rest to your imagination.

By purchasing my supplies in or around my neighborhood, by indulging myself with a lamp and coffee capsules from the very shrines where the top brass of Paris worship, not only was I making my life simpler, I was also, in a way, making my entry into a world that was worthy of my luxurious apartment. My lovely, divine nest. My little Versailles.

In any case, I reassured myself, my savings were substantial. For fifteen years I had held positions in banks of renown. For fifteen years I had been making a good living, climbing the ladder, earning my stripes, reaching salary levels that

would have made my late father's head spin, and that of
Arlette along with it.[1] Fifteen years without having to pay any
rent, or any sort of utility bill. Apart from the odd luxury
clothing item I would buy myself during the sales, I'd hardly
contributed to the food shopping and even more rarely to the
parcels destined for my sister's children, that is, the walled-up-
alive sister in Blida.

"Keep your money," said my mother. "You'll need it when
the time comes."

The time had come, but not in the way my poor mother had
intended, for at that time she had no idea how much I earned,
and if she were apprised now of the objects of my expenses,
she would throw a fit. My mother had been hoping that my
savings would go to the purchase of a villa in a posh suburb—
But not too far from Saint-Ouen, apple of my eye, she intimated.
And of a Renault Espace—I would like four grandsons, my
sweet, so that my home will echo with their cries. Not to mention all the rest—a diamond necklace, solid gold bracelets, a
belt of gold coins, bolts of silk and satin, caftans of velvet
embroidered with gold . . . and so on and so forth.

Offerings that would really impress all the guests from
Saint-Ouen and Blida, thought my mother, filled with delight.

And even if I were to comply with my family's wishes, and
be a slave to their desires, what sort of name was I to give my
children? Mohamed or Pierre? Fatima or Marie? What sort of
upbringing would they have? The same as that of my family—
pious and respectful, which would toss them back and forth
between humiliation and learning centers for at-risk
teenagers. Or my own, newly revised—with neither god nor
master, which in all likelihood would isolate them from my
family and, consequently, from their origins, something

[1] Arlette Laguiller, of course, the Trotskyist politician (Mohamed).

which, probably, surely, would send them from one psychiatric clinic to the next.

Curly locks, curly locks.

So no family, then. That way, I could kick the bucket from cirrhosis of the liver, all alone, on a hospital bed in Blida or in Bichat, or from a heart attack between the thighs of a blonde, in my bedroom with its alcoves, or in a suite in the Bahamas, and my disappearance would affect no one. Is that not the very essence of freedom?

So no family, then, I said again, out loud. Too bad, mother of mine. It's fate, mother dear. It has been written. My mother. My mother sticking to her son. My own sticking skin, mother of mine, ineluctably, must come unstuck from yours.

On that note, he said, I closed my diary and went over to the balcony. I lit a cigarette and leaned my elbows on the balustrade. But no matter how I thought about all the lovely things in store, that rosy light which had enveloped me at the time of the owner's call had not yet managed to reach my inner core.

My mind was now absorbed by trivial considerations: I would die of hunger, for I had never in my life so much as gone near a gas stove. I would go moldy in the dust, for I had never placed a finger on a vacuum cleaner "on" button. I would become mired in filth, for I had never held a sponge in my hand. And who would iron my shirts and trousers? Who would darn my socks? Who would sew the buttons on my shirts? Who would brush my coats and my suits? Who would polish my shoes and my boots?

So I turned my thoughts to frozen food and the microwave oven. And to brasseries—no longer could anyone or anything prevent me from eating there as often as I liked. And a cleaning woman, who would come once a week . . .

And hadn't my cousin Driss lived on his own since arriving in France, a good twenty years ago now, finishing his higher education, setting up the perfect company, signing contracts with renowned multinationals, traveling the world over, from China to the Emirates, offering his genitors a three-story house with bulletproof doors and a sophisticated alarm system, in Algiers on the Corniche de Saint-Eugène, and also a checking account in foreign currency, in the largest Algerian bank, and regular trips to Mecca . . . Driss the lucky devil, Driss blessed by his family, praised by my own, Driss who was accountable to no one. Not even his own person, so he said.

Driss the *bigamist*, two legitimate marriages, consecrated according to ritual, before Allah and before man, with savvy modern women, docile and independent, one a pharmacist, much older than he was, she had loved him and supported him during his studies, the other a professor of ancient Greek, fresh and sweet like Ronsard's rose, according to my cousin. Both of them were *from the home country*, but born on French soil; the girls *from there*, he said, with the exception of the real village yokels, or the veiled ones, hijab-wearing fanatics, were too rebellious, too political to run a household.

So two legitimate spouses. Who, he continued, just like Madame Mitterrand and Mademoiselle Pingeot, shared the same man without a scandal, shared my cousin, who liked to call them "the Mothers." Three or four children. Maybe five. What did he know? Since there was always one on the way, he trumpeted. He need hardly look at either of them, he boasted, nine months later they were ringing him up from the maternity ward.

In short, two families—one on the right bank, the other in a chic suburb not far from Paris—and he kept them both with largesse of means, equity of treatment, regular, well-organized visits, vacations in the mountains and on the Pacific, cultural and linguistic visits with Grandpa and Grandma on the Corniche de Saint-Eugène . . .

A life as regular as clockwork, which in no way cramped my cousin's style and allowed him to put his bachelor flat to good use—it was a superb apartment in the Bastille district, with a view on the Seine, and where he entertained those he called his "concubines," girls *from the home country*, but neither the village yokel nor the hijab-wearing sort, no, real hot, rebellious types, who didn't give a fig about a religious ceremony, and my cousin pampered them like queens, and he showed them off on a regular basis, whenever he gave one of his sumptuous parties in his splendid apartment, complete with caterer and Andalusian or Kabyle or Chaâbi orchestra, or a famous DJ . . . Parties which generally ended up as orgies, even in the middle of Ramadan.

Really high-class orgies, my man, the kind you'd never imagine in your wildest dreams, he bragged, eyeing the goatee which, in those days, surrounded my lips, in keeping with the *sira* of the Prophet. Have you ever seen me drink alcohol or eat pork? Or hook up with a *roumia* who, regardless of the call of nature to which she has responded, leaves the toilet without first purifying her lovely buttocks? he said indignantly whenever I, good Muslim that I was, tried to remind him of the consequences of his transgressions.

"As for Ramadan and prayer," continued my cousin, "never mind if I don't enter Paradise through the gate reserved for those who fast or those who pray, there will be another gate open to me, on the scale of my good deeds, inshallah, I leave Ramadan and prayer to potential amnesiacs and minds without imagination. I personally do not need to go into contortions five times a day to remember that God exists, or starve myself to remember the annual *zakat*. Do you know that ten percent of my annual revenue goes to the poor, and that's not including all the little contributions here and there that fill up those piggy banks at the bakery, and all the offerings at the mosque.

"I don't know if our grandfather taught you, or what they've put into your head out in your suburb, cousin, but just so you know," he quibbled, in his big-shot manner, "in our religion sex pleads not guilty, and so I'm allowed to copulate my fill here on earth, and beyond, inshallah, after my demise. I am not some priest or even some lay Catholic who feels guilty for getting hard whenever he watches the Rexona commercial, nor am I a Rabbi who screws his old lady through a hole in the sheet; I'm a Muslim who is obligated to devote himself to the pleasures of the flesh, which are not a transgression, as you imply, but an offering from the Almighty," he ranted, growing ever more indignant.

And then he burst out laughing: "It's about time for you to start, old man, time to be a man, a real one, and time you began practicing so you'll be able to honor your *houris* who, I am sure, are ready and waiting for a good-looking guy like you. As my favorite proverb has it, in order to satisfy the pearls in Paradise, let us satisfy the ordinary ones here on earth. A little *bismillah*, and bingo! No one's the wiser, and no one will be punished!

"Life's too short, cousin . . . "

I tossed out my cigarette, he continued, and focused my attention on the passersby who, as it was a Saturday in summer and major sales were under way, were swarming along the street, clogging up the sidewalk cafés and flocking into the shops. Not very many mommies were to be seen, not many strollers, in any case. Civilized women think about other things than just procreating right down to the last gamete.

Without the back-street abortionist of our neighborhood in Blida—

I learned what I am about to relate at my own expense, in a Turkish bath or at a marriage, when I was only six or seven years old, where my mother, underestimating a child's unfailing memory, allowed me to mingle with the women and overhear their sordid discussions, and later, when my twin sister, before her wedding and expatriation, was debating her pregnancy I heard her assert, in so many words, that *our* religion allowed abortion before the end of the fourth week of gestation (and without the pill manufactured in our neighborhood, in Saint-Ouen)—as I was saying, without the back-street abortionist of our neighborhood in Blida, my educated and civilized mother (for that is how she described herself) would have engendered something like ten children.

From the age of sixteen, like a good eldest son, to help feed my mother's brood, raise the brothers and marry off the sisters as quickly as possible, I would have had no choice other than to roll up my sleeves, grit my teeth, and, like my father, spend my entire (short) life on the assembly line, fastening bolts onto future automobiles that neither he nor I would ever own.

And farewell to my studies.

Farewell to the good jobs.

Farewell to the well-padded savings account.

Farewell to the lovely nest.

Farewell to poetry and the song of the blackbird.

Farewell to steamy nights . . .

And thus it went with my cogitations until a voice I had thought long gone, along with my erstwhile faith, whispered into my right ear: "And what if, by creating this distance with your family, you were to find yourself endlessly drifting? And what, if by renouncing your loved ones, you were sinking deeper and deeper into a bottomless pit? A pit from which even God himself with the help of his very best saints cannot dislodge you?"

Shit, I swore, feeling myself falter, ready to climb over the balustrade, when the other voice, the adversary of the first one, a voice that has never left me, that was there when I was staring at the dome of the Invalides, into my left ear did whisper: "Have no fear, Arab. With or without God, you are escaping from the she-wolf who was devouring you limb by limb. With or without God, you will be like the baby scorpion that devours its mother just after its birth. And do not forget this, you have just been born. Don't spoil it all, Arab."

Too true. Too true, I found myself saying, deliriously, thinking again of the spasms that had caused me to double over the day I was putting the phone down to go to the real-estate agency.

A sudden joy subsequently dismissed all my dark thoughts, gradually procuring a feeling of lightness I had never before experienced. Neither on the day when I passed my baccalaureate exams with flying colors and found myself with a

scholarship, nor on the day when I came first in my gradu-
ating year at business school and was swamped with proposi-
tions from headhunters . . .

A sensation so intense that I had a knot in my throat. So
intense that I felt like shouting, screaming for joy from the
height of my balcony.

I am a sparrow hawk grazing the summits. I am an eagle
soaring among the stars. I am a star burning without end. I am
eternal. I am a free man.

But I didn't shout or scream for joy.

What would my neighbors think?

That they had a madman in their midst?

My neighbors would inform the concierge posthaste, and
she, in turn, discreet and efficient, would slip a note to the
agency . . .

I did not even dare think of what would ensue—termina-
tion of my lease, return to the slum belt, above all the tri-
umphant breasts of one Mademoiselle Agnès Papinot as she
took my key chain off me and recommended the acquisition of
a hovel, Mademoiselle Papinot whose grandfather or great-
uncle or perhaps even both of them—I have no idea why,
maybe because of her name,[1] or her natural blondness, or the
cold glare of her eyes—I could easily envisage, fifty years or so
ago, shoving Jews into railroad cars bound for Auschwitz. Just
as I could imagine her father and her own self watching the
evening news and applauding *our* lawmakers for shoving *those
foreigners* into charter flights bound for their respective
banana republics, of the totalitarian or socialist people's republic ilk—like the one in which I came into the world, and where
I whiled away my childhood under the protection of the holy
burnous of my august ancestor.

---

[1] Which made me think not of Denis Papin the physicist but of the other
bloke, Maurice Papon, the acolyte of Marshal Pétain (Mohamed).

Having given myself a thorough fright, he said, I decided to keep quiet, and my imagination gradually took another course. Propelled into a near future a few months, at most a year, down the road, the time to put my book together, my imagination entered a world of sound and glitter, of spotlights and movie cameras. Renowned poet, outstanding author, to the world did I hear myself declare:

According to ancestral tradition, until my marriage I should have continued to live—tied to her apron strings—between the four walls of the woman who gave birth and life to me. Thank you, mother of mine. But one day, as I was staring at the dome of the Invalides, a question as resistant as a virus began to nag me. Who am I (if not a shadow)? Who am I (if not a man in chains)? And so on until I realized that I had nothing in common anymore with my loved ones. And all that remained for me to do was to go over the wall, with the firm intention of becoming an individual who decides and charts his life as a Westerner on a full-time basis, with every right thereto pertaining. To sum up, and spare you any useless gloss, I invite you, dear readers, to discover the adventures of a man of forty

a former Islamist

demagogue and virgin

somewhat careerist, but oh dear reader, he is liberating himself from his mother. His mother whom he loves with all his heart.

For—and I insist upon this point—until what was meant to happen did happen, I loved my mother. Loved her like a madman. I was prepared, for her sake, to throw myself from a cliff. Under a train. Blow myself up with dynamite on Mars. If she asked me to.

Prepared for anything.

Hence the anxiety that tore at me as I was leaving her. Hence the sacrifice of my youth, for her sake. Hence the lack of interest I showed my father, and my shame on his behalf, which I have evoked here above, but also the shame which devastated me whenever he had to meet with my teachers, or on the rare occasions when he waited for me outside school and I felt pinned to the ground, and I had to look away, and then I would leg it until I was breathless, straight into my mother's arms, and she would dry my tears and order me to pretend my father—my father, my genitor, the founder of my days of my life—was *someone else.*

The gardener, improvised my mother, brilliantly. Perfectly. Sent by your *father*, who's a businessman, who's very busy, always away on business trips . . .

And I obeyed my mother. Because, as soon as everyone was asleep, no sooner had she finished tidying the kitchen, preparing the breakfast, my father's lunch box, and my snack—the cafeteria at school was beyond our means, so I stole out to eat in the Parc Monceau or in a square not far from the school building—my mother spent the rest of her night bent over a sewing machine.

In addition to the special orders she filled for neighbors, to help make ends meet, for us, for her eldest son in particular, she would reproduce outfits that she had seen in magazines or in luxury boutiques . . . She did so in such a way that, dressed like the nabob that I clearly was not, none of my schoolmates could call into question the *profession* of my father, who, I am now sure of this, had been perfectly aware of my hostility.

Come, my son, come, my blood, come to retrieve my shame, lamented Corneille.

Come, my father, come, my blood . . .

Curly locks, curly locks.

S peculating upon my future as a poet, he continued, light as foam, I had a last stroll around my apartment and then I went out. As I waited for the elevator, I began to hum the tune "He's a free man, Max . . . " then stopped once I arrived on the ground floor. Like any good concierge, my new concierge—forty-something, neither tall nor short, neither slim nor chubby, wearing a T-shirt and a pair of jeans, olive skin, nose somewhat flat, eyes big and dark, hair long and wavy—left her loge and came out to greet me. I introduced myself and gave her my card with my "white" name, correctly spelled.

After she had read it, without a trace of an accent—like any good Frenchman paralyzed by clichés, abetted by her complexion and her first name (Madame Lisa, so Mademoiselle Papinot had told me), I expected her to utter hissing sounds, à la Portuguaise—she informed me of the time of the mail distribution, and the garbage collection, and showed me where the garbage cans were stored, emphasizing that in this building we were required to sort our garbage.

She welcomed me to the building, then gave me the phone number to her loge, and also her cell phone, and said that I could call her in an emergency, that she lived in the neighborhood, and she added that if I needed someone to clean the apartment she could take care of it herself. I acquiesced. Was she not discreet and efficient, I said to myself, envisaging the round firm quivering breasts of Mademoiselle Agnès Papinot.

After I had taken down her telephone numbers in my cell phone, I gave her the extra set of keys. As she was taking them, I noticed the state of her left palm—red and swollen, cracked and oozing. I was about to go back on our agreement, but then abstained.

Scarcely able to hide my disgust, I said, "Bleach?"

"Among other things."

"You must wear gloves, and use ointment. My mother uses—"

"Nothing seems to help," she interrupted with a smile.

Showing me the palm of the other hand, smooth and healthy as a baby's, she added, "When it's all over, the right hand looks just like the left."

"When it's all over?"

But I had no intention to dally over the cutaneous concerns of a little concierge, so I did not leave her time to answer my question, and informed her that her tasks, in my house, would be limited to house cleaning, and that I took my meals out.

"Like most bachelors," she said, bordering on a familiarity that I did not appreciate. "But please, avoid throwing parties, that's not the sort of thing that's done in this building," she added, with a faint pout.

"Fine," I said.

I left the building, not knowing where my feet would take me. I was going to head right, toward the parking lot on the rue de Sèvres, to pick up my car and go back to Saint-Ouen, but in fact I turned left, and found myself on the rue de Rennes. Right before I reached the boulevard Saint-Germain, I stopped outside the Montblanc boutique. And what about treating myself to a new pen, to celebrate my new life? One of those fine black pens with a top embellished in white, of the kind displayed by my cousin and various television presenters?

I searched the window, with its tones of black and white, then told myself that there was no rush. That henceforth this shop was only a few strides from my house, and that right at the moment what was called for was a pleasant spot to mop up my emotions.

On the rare occasions when I had been to the Café de Flore, with Driss or my sister, the disowned one, we had sat inside or upstairs. The terrace is for yokels and tourists, said Driss, sipping on his non-alcoholic cocktail. If you want to see the *gauche caviar* close up, and that of Marrakesh—those specialists on equality who have not yet guillotined their king, who have relegated Léon Blum to oblivion, as well as the couturier from Dior and the philosopher and his doll—avoid the terrace, said my sister.

That particular day, I only had eyes for the boulevard; I wanted to appreciate it, feel sorry for the people packed into buses or standing in crowd in the taxi queue, all these people who were merely passing through Saint-Germain. Des Prés. Whereas I. Only a few minutes (on foot) from my apartment. From my very own home. Because I had *my very own home*. Roughly eight hundred square feet all for me. For me alone. Like a grown-up, I continued, jubilant when I saw a free spot on the terrace. Too bad if I'm not sitting across from the philosopher with his Barbie doll, or from Pierrot the Muscovite, formerly the advisor to the resigning socialist, who lives on your street, or that creator of anorexics, the man from Hamburg with his dark glasses, his buttocks once made of sausages and caviar and who is so proud now to display and to sell his new and quite unexpected thinness.

I was going to order a Météore, the house beer, and then I thought about a mojito, a Cuban cocktail which, if the bartender is the least bit free with his hands when dosing the rum, can sandblast your throat and burn your synapses.

Fearful of returning to my family home drunk, I had never imbibed any strong liquor, hardly allowing myself a beer or two, and I would mask the smell by chewing on sweets. And even this was fairly recent, and only in the company of my sister. For although my cousin may have accepted my religious fanaticism, exhorting me moreover to live "like a man, a real man," I could not be so sure of his tolerance with regard to my newest forms of excess.

Not long thereafter I was savoring my mojito while making a few calls. I called my sister first, and asked her to forward my mail to number such-and-such on the rue Saint-Placide, 75006 Paris. "Incredible!" she exclaimed as I dictated the address to her. "Oh, fancy that! Eight hundred square feet! My brother finally standing on his own two feet! I can't wait to visit your place. Do you know we're almost neighbors? And sometimes I walk over to Le Bon Marché? And you know Pierrot took his infant swim classes nearby, on the rue Notre-Dame des Champs, at the Stanislas swimming pool? The very place where I did my prenatal prep? Remember, I told you about this old midwife who gave us relaxation classes, and who befriended me just because I was the wife of a TV star, and after Yvon's documentary about Algiers she came up to me and said, 'Your husband ought to be a bit wary of Algerians, Madame de Montélimard. He ought to be reminded that those people have hated us since 1830. They will never like us. They'll do their very best to destroy us. And anyway, they have sworn to colonize us in turn. And do you know what weapon they have found to show us they mean business? The uterus! It's just as I tell you, Madame de Montélimard. The uterus. Just look at all their kids, all those Moameds and Moulouds, disgracing our suburbs.' And never once did that old bag suspect my origins. Either she had a serious problem with her eyesight, or else she could not imagine that an Arab, even one with as Zoubida a name as mine, could possibly live in such a place, let alone be the wife of a celebrity with a handle to his name! Oh, my dear little brother finally on his own two feet! I can't get over it. Does the old lady know about it? Oh, dear, well good luck. I've still got such bad memories, you know . . . But it won't be the same for you. Well, let's hope everything will go smoothly. Oh my God, fancy that! Not only are you getting out of there, you're headed somewhere really special . . . Bravo. Really, bravo, brother."

She went on and on, my disloyal sister; she was over the moon and she took the news of my departure as a victory over those who, ten years earlier, without actually putting her on a plane, had disowned her and banished her forever from their life. And what if the same fate befell me? I suddenly wondered.

Driving such an improbable outcome from my thoughts as quickly as I could, I continued my phone calls. By the second mojito, I had informed four or five people that I was moving to Paris—among them Driss, now on vacation in La Rochelle with his latest conquest, possibly a future concubine, a girl from the desert, native of Biskra, hot as a brasero, straight out of a novel by André Gide, delicious earthy nourishment, cousin, he had confided before his departure; and then Gad, with his wife and son, currently visiting an uncle in Casablanca; and then that poor Nawar, who was out walking his matron's mutt, and who was happy to learn that we would henceforth be neighbors. Into a very nice apartment. Only a few cable lengths away from Saint-Germain. Des Prés. Obviously. And to celebrate the event, I would host a dinner. Yes. Yes . . .

Only four or five people. In the name of the life of a recluse. Five years studying, fifteen years working, and so few people in my life. How could there have been more, under my mother's thumb, obliged to respect her curfew? virtually forbidden from going out on Saturday night? with Sunday lunch on the verge of the sacred? even obliged to cancel any trips away from

Paris or abroad? in order to spare the woman who gave me life from her dread of car accidents or plane crashes? *What would become of me if you were to disappear, apple of my eye?*

My mother, the she-wolf who eats her young alive.

I took a big slurp from the third mojito and promised myself I'd make up for lost time. Henceforth, I was committed to catching up, and the list of my friends would grow longer. I would organize parties at my place and go to all those I was invited to.

Only four or five people. And only men. Old classmates from business school, who only knew me by my birth name, like my cousin Driss, and who sometimes called me Momo; colleagues, like Gad or Christian the poet, who only referred to me by my white name, and who were totally ignorant of the original one. Only Nawar knew everything about me, or almost everything. Encouraged by his own life story, I had shared with him some of my own, among other things my family name and my reasons for replacing it—but nothing about private matters, my sexual abstinence, first desired then endured, or my obligations toward my mother. But since I knew that his wife bossed him around, it was clear to me that he would never cross the threshold of my abode. Let alone for a dinner party.

And if I did go ahead and organize a dinner party, well, I'd be in for a fine muddle, and a slew of teasing from some of the recalcitrant ones, my curly locks for example, about any change in their administrative identity, and they might qualify the deed as a renunciation of my origins.

Take Driss, who had not found employment that was worthy of his degrees, was then helped by his first wife, and had eventually set up his own research consultancy: for him, a name change would be tantamount to genocide, so he said. An ethnic war against himself, or something like that. Even if he'd been black like Mobutu, or short like Napoleon (who, by the way, had also Gallicized his name), Driss Ben Mokhtar would have needed no one. And no one would come and hassle him, he said. And he was neither black nor short, but white and tall, as handsome as Zizou (Zidane) and Tomer (Sisley) put together—either one of whom had needed to renounce their origins in order to succeed, he added pointedly.

But I was no star. I had no footwork and I wasn't the least bit funny. Nor did I have a research consultancy, or even an ordinary non-profit association, much less a patroness with a sizeable cash register.

I was a mere financier—a top-level one, to be sure, but still just an employee. Incapable even of pulling strings to get my brother a job in the bank, with his little curls and his little beard. And I was a bachelor to the marrow. My book, on the other hand, will be signed with my birth name, and thus the apostate that I have become will obtain absolution from his loved ones—so went my sudden thoughts.

I feared the onset of a new bout of anxiety, he said, and so I amused myself by regretting that I had not chosen a name like Moses, for example. All for Momo, all for Momo. Tocquard, Momo. Momo Tocquard. You can smell the imposter a mile away. And why not Maurice? Like Audin, for example.[1] Momo for all, all for Momo. But it was too late.

So no dinner, then. Or a dinner with new people. At the age of forty, I could still make friends. I would no longer need to resort to relatives, like Driss, whom I've kept in my life for lack of anyone better. Anyway, I would see. And such a minor detail, for goodness' sake, was not about to spoil my first hours if not as a free man at least as one about to be free.

I began to stare at the women who came into the café, to single out the prettiest ones, imagining, like a feline on the hunt, which ones would succumb to my Greek profile and my athletic allure.

For a moment I thought I recognized Mademoiselle Papinot, and my heart skipped a beat. I watched my real-estate agent's double as she sat down at the table to my right. Just as she was settling in her chair our eyes met: hers were shining with a joyful glow, mine with the desire to bite right into her. But her gaze, as if I were transparent, as if my six feet and my

[1] Mathematician and member of the Algerian Communist Party, he was assassinated by the French Army for his activities in favor of an independent Algeria. Quite recently and without ceremony, his name was given to a little square off of the rue des Ecoles, in the 5th arrondissement (Mohamed).

hundred and eighty-five pounds had suddenly evaporated, departed for other horizons.

Too bad for you, young lady, you don't know what you're missing, I said to myself, careful not to blow my cigarette smoke straight into her face.

By the fifth pretty girl and the fourth mojito, I was anesthetized, my palate totally insensitive to the rum and fresh mint. Only the taste of lime was still perceptible.

Better stop there before my brain was anesthetized—plus I had to drive. I thought about going home in a taxi, but then I remembered I needed the car the next day for my little move. For who, in the name of luxury, could stay away from little Versailles for more than twenty-four hours? I thought, looking at my watch.

The Monoprix on the rue de Rennes did not close until ten P.M., so I had plenty of time to stretch my legs and refresh my head among its cool shelves. I'd take the opportunity to stock up on mineral water, wine, and whisky, on soap powder and detergent, on noodles and canned food, and have it all delivered on Monday morning. Rue Saint-Placide. In the 6th arrondissement. Yes, please, I would say, with restraint.

And then, drawing closer to the ear of the employee—no doubt a dark-faced immigrant from the land that I had abandoned forever, some guy who would respect Ramadan and his mother—I would abandon all restraint and whisper, Me run away. You heard me, bro, got the hell out. Yes, yes. But me, comrade, me have means to take off, I end up among cream of the crop, who make their butter from your nothing status as never whitened.

In high spirits, I waved to the waiter, and called my mother to warn her I'd be late. An urgent case, I lied. The way I sometimes lied, though quite rarely.

Oh, no! shrieked my mother, while I paid the bill with my credit card.

Just a little bit late, I was murmuring, when my gaze landed upon the figure of the young woman sitting at the table on my left, in such a way that she was in perfect symmetry with the real estate agent's double who, given the way she analyzed the male patrons who came into the café, must have been waiting for a blind date.

As for the young lady on my left, she must have been there for quite a while already—her wine glass was nearly empty—and, given the concentration with which she was reading her newspaper, she wasn't waiting for anyone, I deduced to my satisfaction.

Maybe I won't even have any dinner, I murmured then, observing her discreetly.

Thirty years old or so, dark as the devil, almost black, long wavy hair, sober but elegantly dressed in jeans with a white shirt, something familiar and reassuring emanated from her person.

While my mother continued to lecture me—how could I leave her in the lurch like that, on a Saturday evening, not only had she gone to the bother of making pancakes, but I was supposed to go the next morning early to the market at Saint-Denis; my sister (the blessed one) and her husband (the convert) were back from their honeymoon and were coming over for lunch—I looked right at the young woman's face. Her nose was somewhat flat, her eyes were big and dark, her lips slightly too fleshy, not a trace of makeup, not even the residue of some lipstick or kohl that she might have put on that morning . . .

You wouldn't say she was beautiful, exactly, and nothing in her face matched my taste. But no doubt because of the solitude that was starting to bedevil me, and the rum that made it all the sharper, I could not take my eyes off her.

She eventually noticed, and raised her gaze from her paper and directed it at me. A gaze that was hard and frightened at the same time. A gaze that is peculiar to Arab women, one I've seen on the face of my mother my sisters my cousins my would-be fiancées, and I picked up on it immediately.

I gave her a faint smile, but she was already folding up her paper and calling the waiter. Instead of asking to pay, as I had thought she would, she wanted to order. The same thing, she said, winking at me, furtively, to be sure, but as eloquently as can be, indicating not only that she was staying but also that she was waiting for some sign from me to get acquainted. I was quivering. But fearful that I might have been mistaken, preferring to intercept some additional sign of encouragement, I did not venture anything.

And given the poise with which she carried herself, with which she called the waiter, and of the wink with which she had subtly gratified me, I had a sudden doubt. What if she wasn't Arab at all, what if she were merely some white woman who had just returned from vacation, her skin gorged with sun?

What on earth would I do with a white woman who didn't even look like a white woman? I wondered, while she was rummaging in a plastic bag from the La Hune bookstore. A moment later she was holding a book with the most morbid cover imaginable, the photo of a woman who looked anything but alive. I managed to read the name of the author—a woman, an Arabic name of the Middle Eastern variety, someone I'd never heard of. The title, *Djamila and Her Mother,* with the help of my mother's voice, momentarily became *Mohamed and His Mother.* Suppressing a laugh, I swore I had to meet the woman who'd written such a thing.

In short, I continued to observe the young woman who was now reading the summary of the book with an almost joyful expression on her face, as if she were congratulating herself for her purchase, and I was no longer listening to my mother.

An Arab, I thought, she must be one of those somewhat

rebellious Algerian types. Only Algerian rebellious types could joyfully endure books with such sinister covers, and given the café and the bookstore she hangs out in, she had to be from the intellectual middle class in Algiers.

As a student I'd come across a few girls like her, little daddy's girls, proud and inaccessible, who came to Paris for their studies and spent their time living it up. They were far too noxious for my convictions at the time, and I avoided them and condemned them with all the fervor I possessed, multiplying my dose of prayers to send those Satanic creatures to rot in hell. A believer like myself would enjoy the seventy *houris* promised by Allah: that was my consolation, and whenever they passed before me, I lowered my gaze.

Those days were well behind me now, and my faith had been irrevocably lost, so this girl had come along at just the right time to enliven a few of my evenings on the rue Saint-Placide: those were my thoughts while my mother continued her desperate soliloquy.

Just as I was hanging up, the young woman detached her gaze from her reading and directed it once again at me. Her gaze was hard and frightened at the same time, though I could detect a smile.

A few hours later, said he, at around one o'clock in the morning, I came in and closed the door of the apartment in the Saint-Ouen projects. Without switching on the light, I put down the bag full of your books—which I had just bought at La Hune, for the bookstore was open until midnight, or so I had realized with delight upon entering—then I untied my laces and thought back on the nice little evening that I had spent in the company of my first conquest, not yet possessed, but the labyrinths of whom I had the firm intention of exploring. Clefts and slits. Etc.

For our first encounter, given the lack of furniture in my abode, and because the moment did not seem apposite, and as on all the (rare) times that I had gone up to a woman—thanks in particular to my sister who was in a hurry to see me leave the four walls of our "old lady" behind—I was content merely to listen to her.

With grace and levelheadedness—her eyes, her lips, her nose that up to now I had not fully appreciated, grew lovelier by the minute—she told me about the life she used to lead in Algiers. And then the circumstances, ten years ago now, which had compelled her to leave—fear, blood, the random nature of things, she said. Without any particular emphasis or pathos.

She suddenly stopped talking about herself and began to show an interest in me. What did I do in life, where did I live? For the same reasons that prevent me from knowing why I found her moving, when I had patently decided only to dally with white women—whatever Driss's views on the matter—I don't know why I omitted to talk about Saint-Ouen. I claimed that I had always lived in this neighborhood, around the 7th or 6th arrondissement, and I left things utterly ambiguous regarding the actual date of my arrival in France. All I told her was that originally I was from Blida.

She said, "Oh, the city of Roses and of Jean Bensaïd also known as Jean Daniel. But now, alas, it is the capital of the Triangle of Death. You know . . . "

I knew, because my sister, the walled-up one, lived there, in the Triangle of Death, and because my family, since my father's death, but also because everything was going up in flames, had gone less and less often to visit and finally stopped going altogether—but I kept silent about these details, and about my father's profession and his death and the circumstances thereof, and about my relationship with my mother, and my brother's little beard and his friends from the mosque, and my former life as a "good Muslim," and the plans I had for my book. And about my white name, as well. I did let her think that white blood flowed in my veins, inherited from a Norman grandmother, whom my grandfather is supposed to have met during the Second World War and whom he brought to Algeria.

To which she replied by alluding to my "fairly typical physique, all the same." Which left me speechless, sending me back to the memory of Mademoiselle Papinot's eyes and then the evanescent gaze of her double, still seated on my right, sipping on her drink with her eyes trained on the door.

To change the subject I began to talk about the history of the café: Sartre, Beauvoir, Boris Vian, Juliette Gréco . . .

She knew all that, she said, laughing in my face. She hadn't been buried in a cave, she was from Algiers the White, the city where, along with other world monuments, Montherlant had found refuge and asserted his misogyny, she said with a smile, and she informed me that she had a degree in modern literature and that, in any case, for *us,* for Algerians, Paris held no secrets. Nor did the language of Voltaire, she continued soberly. And she declared, "Algiers was the extension of Paris, and Paris received the waves and echoes of Algiers, as if the sirocco were blowing on the trees of the Tuileries, bringing with it the sand of the desert and the beaches . . . "

"Voltaire?" I asked.

"Modiano," she replied. "Whom I would gladly marry, just as I would gladly marry Marguerite Yourcenar, if she were still here on earth," she added with half a smile.

And thereupon, instead of heading for home to ease my mother's distress, which I imagined must have reached its paroxysm, I switched off my cell phone and invited her for dinner. In quieter surroundings, I suggested. She confessed she only rarely came to the Flore, and each time it was by chance, that the place, despite the presence of the Japanese, was a bit too "white" for her. But as she had to be home by midnight, why not have dinner there after all, she said, lighting a cigarette.

I agreed and we had dinner. I ordered the Welsh rarebit, melted cheese on white bread, the specialty of the café, and she was content with a salad of green beans, although she did not skimp where the choice of wine was concerned. And it was excellent wine, moreover, just as the bill, when it came, was steep.

What was it? I wondered as I hunted for my slippers in the dark apartment. That girl deserved better. Her mere presence in the café had gone a long way toward reinforcing my aptitude for pleasure and wonder. In other words, the little doubt that still subsisted regarding my dissidence, thanks to her, thanks to her own emancipation, not from a mother and a brother, but from an entire society, had vanished without trace.

In addition, her body, through the rhythm of her gestures

beneath her white shirt, seemed to me the most wonderful thing on earth. And when she agreed to see me again, I was that close to jumping for joy (as I anticipated the moment when I would strip her bare)—even though, through the snatches she had revealed about her life, I had matched up dates and added up years and very quickly realized that she must be close to forty. Therefore, instead of keeping it to myself, I shared my calculations with her, chuckling, adding that I was an uncommon financier. Ha, ha.

Her cheeks pink from the wine, and also from my tactless-ness, of which this would not be the only instance, she confirmed that she was forty-four, to be precise. Forty-four! I whistled. Suppressing the phrase that was at the tip of my tongue *(You could be my little sister's mother)*, and clearing my throat, I said, "You don't look it."

Which, as I stated above, was certainly true. But all the same.

Forty-four years old!

A forty-something, I thought, shoving my feet in my slippers. And then, taking hold of my bag of books, I left my chair. Staggering, and trying not to bump into the walls, groping my way about on tiptoes, crossing my fingers that my mother would not suddenly appear and see me in this state of inebriation, I found my way to the hall and made it to the bathroom without incident.

As I was trying to relieve my stomach, unfairly blaming the quality of the cheese, underestimating the number of glasses I had imbibed, I heard steps in the hallway. Immediately afterward, a murmur came through the locked door.

"Apple of my eye, is that you? Are you all right?"

My mother who, obviously, once she was reassured, rebuked me for switching off my cell phone—she had feared the worst, she had been on the verge of calling the police and the hospitals, I had no right to get her into such a state . . .

I went closer to the door and murmured something that might pass for an excuse. And my mother went away again, praising Allah, rendering grace to her deceased, thanking Him for having restored the apple of her eye to her safe and sound. Etc.

When I went into the bedroom, my younger brother's snoring was at its pinnacle. I switched on the little night-light, hid the bag of books under the bed, and began to get undressed. As I slipped on my pajamas, I thought about my apartment, and my future life, and then I thought again about the forty-something's body. And about our next, imminent, meeting. For, despite my tactlessness, not only had she accepted to see me again, but also, or so it seemed to me, this meant to her that we had laid the foundations of some sort of relationship.

It goes without saying that I had no intention of having anything lasting with her. Or with anyone else, for that matter. My objective was, as I have already pointed out, to have my way with as many women as possible. To have relationships as brief as they were volcanic. To immerse myself in debauchery and luxury. Unto satiety, I said again, carefully folding my clothes. Until depletion. Of the senses. And of that store of hormones that each man owes it to himself to evacuate.

It was then that I remembered she had not told me her first name. Let alone her family name. And that she had not given me her telephone number. However, she had taken mine down. My cell phone number. And what if, after all that, she didn't contact me?

Suppressing a desire to smoke, I swallowed a Stilnox and switched off the night light. As I rehashed my day, sleep took over at the point where Mademoiselle Papinot's breasts began to quiver like young pigeons . . .

I was dreaming about a blonde, he said, a blonde with firm round breasts, when my mother pulled open the curtains. "Good morning, apple of my eye," she said.

Still queasy from all the mojitos and Bordeaux of the previous night, and fearful of the whiffs of rum and wine in my mouth, I kept silent and closed my eyes, with no aspirations beyond a delicious lie in.

"It's almost nine o'clock," she said, just as I was pulling the sheet over my face and begging for a moment of respite.

"Your sister and brother-in-law are coming for lunch," she reminded me.

"I worked all night long," I muttered through the sheet.

"Mahmoud has been up since the first prayer," went my mother, with a note of reproach in her voice.

I mustered all my strength and dragged myself out of bed. In a fraction of a second I had picked up my clothes, deposited a semblance of a kiss on my mother's forehead, and headed through the apartment to the bathroom.

After I had showered and brushed my teeth thoroughly, I went into the kitchen where my brother, with his elbows on the table, was immersed in reading the yellowing pages of a Hadith book of saints, one that I myself had bought, some years earlier, at the Avicenne bookshop in the 5th arrondissement.

My mother served me a coffee and I sat down across from my brother. Without lifting his eyes from his book, he replied to my good morning. I drank my coffee and took a good look at him in his outfit for the mosque—skullcap, baggy pants, and tunic in the Afghan style, immaculately white—and I felt a sort of need, gratuitous but pressing nonetheless, to lead him astray.

"You want to come with me to the market, brother?" I said.

Somewhat surprised by this sudden and unusual request on my part, placing his hand on his freshly pruned little beard, he said, "I'm already dressed for mosque, you can see that, Mohamed."

"Yes, I see that, little brother," I replied, pretending to be disappointed.

"You don't really expect your brother to hang around the market at Saint-Denis in his Afghan clothes and get himself arrested like some vulgar terrorist, now do you?" interrupted my mother as she handed me the shopping list.

"True enough," I agreed.

"I have yours washed and ironed," said my mother. "You'll put it on when you get back."

Ordinarily I would acquiesce and then find a way, when the time came, to sidestep the issue. But this morning, still addle-brained from my very first libation, I said, "I'm not going to the mosque."

My brother looked up again, opened his eyes wide, then returned to his book.

Dumbfounded, my mother said, "What will your brother-in-law say?"

"Tell him I'm tired."

"And he's not even a Muslim," mumbled my mother.

"He is now," I corrected, directing my gaze toward the jar which stood imposingly on the kitchen buffet.

An erstwhile pickle jar, where now my brother-in-law's fore-skin bathed in formaldehyde, and which my mother had placed on exhibit for neighbors and other close friends who had the nerve, or the tactlessness, to emphasize the fact that her daughter's husband was no more than a *roumi*, thereby reminding her that an alliance of this nature, had her men still been alive, i.e. her husband and her noble father, would never have come about. Had she forgotten the grounds for her elder daughter's expulsion? Or for the banishment of the youngest? What did her sons make of it, then, the elder above all, that specialist on hopeless fatwas without appeal . . .

A *roumi*, but not a *kafir*, my mother would thunder. Converted and circumcised according to the rules. Every bit as Muslim as Yusuf Islam,[1] Muhammad Ali, and Malcolm X, she would enumerate, brandishing the jar.

"Of course he's a Muslim," said my mother, close to moaning. "But if we don't set the example—"

"I am not going to the mosque," I interrupted.

"Yes, apple of my eye," she said, with a lost expression.

"Right, I've got to go do this shopping," I said, getting to my feet.

"Yes, apple of my eye," she said again, and by now her mouth was open, her expression distraught: you might have said the sky was gently falling on her head.

Satisfied that I had been sufficiently firm with the she-wolf, and avoiding the farewells and embraces she habitually bestowed upon me as if I were heading off for the ends of the earth, I left the house.

As I shifted into second gear and lit a cigarette, I wondered when and how I would break the news of my imminent departure.

---

[1] The singer Cat Stevens, revered in many North African families for his conversion to Islam (Mohamed).

By around ten o'clock, he continued, I was unloading the trunk of my old Peugeot. This won't happen again, this is the last time, I ruminated, as I greeted the neighbors who were hanging around in the parking lot. Outside the elevator I smiled at two young girls who were examining me with lust so extreme as to be almost embarrassing. For—need I point it out?—in our neighborhood, despite my forty years or more and my graying temples, I continued to be considered one of the most desirable catches for these young damsels. And, if I am to believe my mother's statistics, or the ones put forward by the Ministry of Integration, there were not very many of us.

No sooner had I crossed the threshold than my mother greeted me as if I had just returned from the ends of the earth, without even giving me time to unburden myself of the shopping, not the least bit spiteful, dismissing my behavior earlier that morning with a wave. Faced with such effusiveness, I again wondered when and how I would break the news of my imminent departure. And, above all, how she would take it.

Why didn't I just leave? Use a trip out of town or abroad as a pretext? Insist upon it. Tell her my rank was at stake, or even my position. Settle in between my four walls. And then announce it to her by telephone? Or in a letter? A long letter, that would place her before the fait accompli.

My mother, who was fairly educated, as I have already pointed out, was crazy about my letters; even the little notes I left for her on the refrigerator sent her into raptures, and she often expressed her nostalgia for the long and carefully written epistles that I used to send to her from summer camp.

I extricated myself from my mother's embrace, put the shopping down at the door to the kitchen, and withdrew to my bedroom. A letter would simplify everything, I said to myself as I stretched out on the bed. Dear mother, sweetest of the sweet of all mothers.

But when all was said and done, the letter was a very bad idea. Because, for my new life, I needed the blessing of the woman who had borne and raised me. And a letter would not elicit that vital blessing.

In a parody of the character of Mario in *La Terrazza*, I chuckled to myself and wondered if it was admissible to be happy, even if it caused others to be unhappy. As the answer was yes, and too bad if there was collateral damage, I dozed off with the memory of the forty-something woman reading with delight the back cover of your book. A book which was now in my possession and which I had every intention of reading, just as I had every intention of devouring the others which were there, among my things, almost all packed and discreetly set to one side.

An hour later I was wide awake, the aroma of couscous was tickling my nostrils, and the young newlyweds were ringing at the door.

My sister was wearing her Sunday dress and headscarf, and her husband, his goatee meticulously trimmed, was sporting the Afghan outfit cut and sewn courtesy of my mother for the purposes of the aforementioned circumcision. An outfit which, I had to admit, applauding in my heart of hearts my younger sister's tastes, suited him to a T, as it emphasized his gray eyes and his smooth—naturally—and shiny black hair.

Squeezing her son-in-law in her arms, calling him *my boooy,* my mother shot me a glance where I thought I could detect a glow of pride. Or of victory. Or, quite simply, she was trying to arouse my jealousy, the way a woman does with her beloved. My mother had been dispossessed of her youth, and to compensate for what had been taken from her she now confused me with the person she should have loved. That man who died the way he had lived, in sadness and solitude: I stumbled upon these thoughts just as the embraces were finally coming to an end. And my heart felt tight, then filled with a sudden vivid aversion toward this woman whose blessing I would very soon have to implore.

The women, he said, as you might have guessed, were busy in the kitchen, while we men sat down with our shoes off in the room reserved for special occasions, a place that seemed undecided between the atmosphere of a harem and that of a prayer room: Berber rugs, mattresses on the floor covered with red velvet, gold-embroidered satin cushions thrown here and there, pink and white copper trays, flamboyant wall coverings, prayer mats ready to be unrolled . . . On the wall there was a single portrait of my father, several of our august ancestor, and pictures of the Kaâba and the mosque in Medina . . . The perfectly ordinary living room of North African immigrants, said I to myself, while my brother painstakingly wedged cushions behind our brother-in-law's back.

Once he too was settled, my brother immediately began his ritual lecture on the dogma and principles of Islam. This was more for my brother-in-law's benefit than mine. In vain, my claims that I performed my prayers at the bank in my office, like a Saudi emir or an Algerian minister—was I not master of my domain, I added, in response to my young brother's incredulous expression—or at the Grand Mosque which was now very near my work. In vain, my efforts to convince them by means of a few genuflections after the evening meal. In vain my tooth-brushing and candy-chewing, whenever I had had a beer or two. In vain my pleas of fatigue to avoid the neighborhood mosque: very quickly my brother had picked up on my loss of interest for everything which, once upon a time, had sealed our complicity, such as reading the Koran and the Hadith, and the apology and analysis of the holy *sharia*, whose laws we would enumerate and discuss.

"Supremely logical," one of us would say.

"Let's take repudiation," continued the other.

"Is that not what a bad wife deserves?"

"And what of the support that women, those fragile creatures, are granted for life?"

"Can you imagine, if our sisters were left to their own devices, in this world of barbarians?"

"And what about polygamy, isn't that what is best about our religion?"

"It's the best way to populate the planet."

"No better way to prevent a man from getting bored with one and the same wife."

"And co-wives, after all, would be a great support to our mother, with all her menial chores."

Thus, while my brother pretended to ignore me, I recalled all the texts we used to read to console ourselves for the chastity we endured unflinchingly—a chastity which we would put an end to soon enough by marrying young. It is a Muslim's duty to procreate as soon as possible, we read, emphatically. Our reading left us enthusiastic to the point of swooning. What marvels awaited men of good faith in the celestial Gardens!

"A coveted place shall pass to pious men by right," one of us would remark.

"In the Gardens there will be good and beautiful virgins, *houris* cloistered in their pavilions," continued the other.

"*Houris* that no man, or demon, has ever touched."

"Beautiful women with ripe breasts, all equally young."

"Beautiful as rubies and coral."

"*Houris* whom we have shaped to perfection."

"Every man shall dispose of seventy alcoves."

"In each alcove there shall be a bed."

"On each bed a *houri* shall await the Chosen One."

"Can you imagine, brother, seventy virgins for one man alone!" we would exclaim, raising our eyes from the Book.

Then we would continue reading, and our reading led us until dawn. It should have led me to marriage with one, or several—what did my cousin Driss have that I didn't have?—of the beautiful women whom my mother had found.

As I was the eldest, it was more according to tradition than to divine law that I ought, by right, to be the first to marry. My future spouse would be chosen, as the Law decreed, in keeping with one of these criteria: beauty, youth, or wealth. The fiancée's religion—unlike that of a fiancé—provided it be one of those of the people of the Book, mattered little.

But this last criterion held no sway over my mother, for she refused to consider a Christian or a Jew, or even a Tunisian or Moroccan woman, let alone a Senegalese. In theory, my mother, as a believer, had nothing against blacks—was not Bilal, the first *muezzin*, a black man? she used to say. But a Negress, an excised woman, my son . . . she winced.

In short, in my mother's eyes, and in her heart, only an Algerian would do. But woe betide any Algerian woman who was older than twenty-two. If they are still single past that age they become depraved, she asserted. It was not for nothing that the holy Koran recommended marriage at puberty, might she remind me. Well, in our day and age, twenty-two was all right, but it was the limit, apple of my eye.

My mother, therefore, had scouted for girls from Blida to introduce to me, as well as others from the countryside, all of them Algerian and barely past adolescence, and they really didn't meet my expectations. Too curly-haired or too dark. A bit too dumb or a bit too smart, I would plead in earnest. More recently, somewhat gingerly, there had been the aforementioned mayor's daughter, who combined all three criteria; her photograph, forwarded by my mother's appointed matchmaker, always seemed by virtue of some mysterious miracle to be lying around in the house wherever I happened to be.

And so, he continued, while my young brother was saying his homilies, I recalled those nights when I would struggle in vain against the demon that led my thoughts toward the lovely Eve and the handsome Adam, obliging my ignoble self to imagine the first creatures of the human race in the process of copulating.

Adam on Eve, Eve on Adam, whispered the demon into my left ear.

And my hand all sticky when I woke up.

And my frantic sprint to the washing machine to hide the stained sheet.

And the voice ringing in my right ear. The same voice that had caught me unawares on the balcony, that I had thought was gone forever. Expiate. Expiate, said the voice, drilling into me, all day long. Expiate, it whispered, while my prayers made me dizzy until dawn.

And my brother, who praised my piety at breakfast. My brother, who slept so soundly and never heard the echo of my ugly thoughts.

All that seemed so long ago that I wondered whether my brother and I were still brothers. Or were we not, rather, a present-day incarnation of Cain and Abel?

Who was Abel?

Who was Cain?

I still cannot say.

But I know that my brother will never forget who was "one" and who was the "other."

Mohamed, alias Basile, the master; Mahmoud the pure, the disciple. But the master lost his grip. From one day to the next. I cannot determine the precise moment when his renunciation began, how it wheedled its way in so successfully. No doubt at the very start of my professional life, when my eyes looked out onto the city, and I discovered the real city and all its mysteries, the real city and its lights. Or earlier, much earlier, at the moment of my father's death, and the revelations which followed. I know not.

And what if, quite simply, I had never possessed the faith. What if it had been nothing more than the product of a long, assiduous education, merely glancing off my soul without ever burning into its fiber? The true fiber, the one you find in people whose souls are unfailing? How, in other words, could a person become so detached from something he had taken to be the very nature of conviction itself, I wondered—while my brother continued his palaver, beatific, as if he himself had converted that *roumi*. An act worth its weight in gold, and which, tomorrow, will prove very profitable to its author.

My brother, he continued, was elaborating on I know not what precept when, discreetly, to avoid disturbing the discussion among the menfolk, my sister came into the room. After spreading a tablecloth onto the coffee table, she withdrew as discreetly as she had entered.

Perhaps, I thought, watching her slip away, this distancing from my brother and from our discourse became inevitable because of the solidarity I felt toward my mother with my sisters with all the pious women on earth who shall not enjoy the equivalent of the seventy *houris*. Who will have to make do with whoever their husband happens to be. And if that husband is not admitted into the Gardens, well then, may they be reassured, affirms the Book: they will marry again, and will marry a Chosen One.

Once they were joined to a Chosen One, whether he was their husband on earth or another one chosen from the innermost recesses of Paradise, it meant that these women, who submitted to Allah and to his men, would share their spouses with the seventy *houris*. Something which, in the end, would constitute a new form of polygamy, even more restrictive and unfair than the one already established on earth. First of all, because of the number of co-wives. Secondly, because of their esthetic qualities, something no Earthling, however beautiful she might be, could ever hope to compete with.

I took a closer look at my brother, who was continuing his palaver, gesticulating, his forehead pearling with sweat, then turned to my brother-in-law, who was listening without saying a thing, without moving a muscle.

And what if Alain also known as Ali had only come to Islam for the flesh and debauchery promised by the Book? And what if, despite his angelic air, this young man now unburdened of his foreskin was nothing more than a sexual pervert? sodomizing my sister? tying her up? gagging her? night after night? day after day? Following to the letter the verse inviting believers to *labor*[1] their wives and unaware, poor neophyte, of the one where sodomy is proclaimed to be strictly off limits.

I then gave a sort of hiccup, like a chuckle, that distracted my brother from his homily.

After a certain amount of time had gone by, and upon ripe reflection, he said, "Would you list for us the ninety-nine names of God?"

I cleared my throat, ready to comply, and then I gave up. My brother, given my silence, grew rather irritated.

"Could it be you have forgotten them, brother?"

I had not forgotten them, and I would never forget them. I could, therefore, list them for him, in due time and in order, and remind him that "Allah" was the hundredth name, and that those Muslims who knew the names would enter Paradise unconditionally.

Just as I could remind him of every name of every angel or demon created by God, from Jibril, the archangel with six hundred wings, councilor and helpmate to the Prophet, to Iblis, the disobedient one, who refused to bow down before man, as embodied by Adam, God's preferred creature. Or I could give him a detailed lecture on the life and conception of the djinns, who were subordinate to Iblis, the same, these creatures who resemble us, who see us, and whom we humans,

---

[1] "Your wives are your field: go in, therefore, to your field as ye will," in the Koran (Mohamed).

with few exceptions, do not see. Or I could give him a lecture on sexuality, while we're at it, which would fortify our brother-in-law upon his entry into the sexiest religion of all, emphasizing all the while the absolute irrevocable prohibition where sodomy was concerned, bro . . .

But I felt no desire to vaunt my erudition, neither for my brother's satisfaction nor to improve the neophyte's knowledge, so I pleaded a headache and, therefore, my inability to fulfill his request.

Ruffled, my young brother turned again to our attentive brother-in-law:

"Mohamed is very clever at religion. He masters the rules and the dogma probably just as well as the Imam el-Ghazali himself. He owes it to our grandfather, may Allah receive him in his Gardens, a good man of great learning, one of the rare men of letters in Blida. He had completed his Islamic studies at the Zitouna, the famous school in Tunis, which unfortunately no longer exists. Once or twice a year his fellow students came from all four corners of the Maghreb to meet him. For days they held meetings which lasted until morning. This is the master who gave Mohamed the teachings of the *Mashaf*, who initiated him into the doctrines of renowned *ulemas* and *faqihs* such as el-Ghazali, and who accompanied him in person to Koranic school every morning at dawn, and also went with him to the public school and insisted that the teachers do a good job teaching him French, because his grandson might be called upon to join his father in France. Not to mention the pre-Islamic poetry, including that of the Andalusian era, that he introduced Mohamed to, quite brilliantly . . . Do you know, my brother Ali, that the Prophet, may peace be upon him, was a passionate admirer of poetry? That the poets came all the way to his dwelling-place to recite their lyrics?"

Our brother-in-law shook his head, and my young brother continued, "Whatever the case, Mohamed is the only one of us who was able to benefit fully from our grandfather's great store of knowledge, and to go to the *madrasah*, and to read and write Arabic like a graduate of the Zitouna."

And he shot me a dark look.

"That's very fortunate, isn't it?"

"Very," I replied, nonchalantly.

"If I had been that fortunate," continued my brother, "today I would be a member of an eminent Sufi brotherhood, like our late lamented grandfather, or a renowned theologian. But I'm still young, and Allah will help me, inshallah, to stay on the straight and narrow," he went on, firing another pitch-black look in my direction.

"Inshallah," I murmured.

"Inshallah," murmured my brother-in-law.

"Unemployment will eventually prove to have a silver lining," said my brother, indefatigably. "I have all the time to read and improve my learning, and one day I will be able to enroll in a great Islamic school in Damascus or Cairo. Inshallah."

"Inshallah."

"Inshallah."

At this juncture, he said, my mother and sister came in. While they were setting the table, my brother got up and switched on the radio, where an Oriental melody was playing. He turned down the volume and came back to join us at the coffee table.

The *bismillah* was recited in unison, and, with the meal blessed, we began our lunch. In the middle of the meal, as was her wont during Sunday dinner, my mother put her spoon down and let out a sigh that was audible enough to cause us to look up from our plates.

"Only your father is missing, may he rest in peace, and my poor daughter in Blida, that hellhole."

My sister, as was her wont, took my mother's hand and with another litany declaimed, "Fatima is doing all right in Blida."

"*Ameen*," whispered my mother, with that expression full of contrition that we knew so well.

"She's been there so long now," added my sister.

"*Ameen*," repeated my mother, her face now crumbling with pain.

"You have to see it as good fortune, mother dear, the fact that she is living in a land of Islam," continued my sister, her voice trembling slightly.

"A country where Muslims kill each other does not qualify as a land of Islam, sister," said my brother at that point, in his professorial tone.

"Don't squeeze my heart more than it has been already, my son," moaned my mother.

And then, as if she were suddenly getting a grip, she removed her hand from her daughter's, picked up her spoon, and said, "If she hadn't insisted on always having her own way, we wouldn't have had to marry her off back there."

"A forced marriage is still a forced marriage," said my brother.

"The fact is that Fatima has held out for more than fifteen years now," added my sister. "Her children are well brought up, and even if he is a bit strict her husband is a good sort."

"Often," said my brother, "if not always, a forced marriage turns out to be more enduring than a so-called love marriage, which is nothing but a Western invention."

My sister looked furtively at her husband, and said nothing more.

"Allah knows best," murmured my mother.

And the lunch continued to the lament of the *oud* on the radio, interrupted now and again by (religious) anecdotes recounted by my brother, then commented upon by my mother with such sincerity and ingenuity that for a moment I thought of giving up my plans to move away. I could call the Sèvres agency on Monday. I could cancel the lease. I could try to get the deposit and the rent checks back. Never mind if they didn't return them. My mother's well-being was worth so much more.

B ut, he said, when the time came for the mint tea, the voice in my left ear banished the tinnitus in my right ear, and I took the plunge.

"I'm going to be moving to Paris," I said, staring at the *makrout* pastries oozing honey and butter.

"Oh, really?" said my brother.

And he choked on his tea. My sister and brother-in-law exchanged a glance and my mother put down her glass and the pastry she had been about to bite into. With her mouth open, she began to stare at her hands as if she were hunting for the words that she couldn't find.

"I'm worn out by the commute to Paris," I improvised.

"Why don't you just transfer back to Saint-Denis," said my brother, slowly chewing his *makrout*.

"I can't . . . "

"You want to leave me, and you're not even married?" said my mother eventually.

"Precisely. First an apartment, and then marriage," I replied hastily.

"That's unheard of," said my brother, wiping his lips.

Looking at our mother, in a lifeless voice he added, "He won't go far, mother. In Paris, they don't rent out apartments to the likes of a Mohamed Ben Mokhtar."

Mohamed Ben Mokhtar alias Basile Tocquard almost burst out laughing at that point. And what if he were to tell them, there and then, on the spot, that he had changed his name? His brother would pass out, his sister and brother-in-law would despise him, and his mother would banish him from her life forever. Or maybe not. Was he not the apple of her eye? Was she not extremely forgiving where her sons were concerned? Golden coins that nothing could sully, as my mother liked to say, whereas her daughters were constant bombs, one day they went boom, right in your face, and it had to be said that she was the one who had had to pay.

Be that as it may, I thought, I shall keep my secret unto death. Until my death or hers.

You will, if the she-wolf devours you down to the last toe. She will, if you turn into the baby scorpion.

As if rushing to my assistance, my brother put an end to my cruel thoughts.

"No matter how you much whiten your skin and straighten your hair," he said scornfully, "your name will always catch up with you."

Somewhat taken aback by such provocation, and ready to do battle, I frowned and clenched my fists. But I refrained. What would the neophyte think of his in-laws? Moreover, my brother and I had never come to blows—at the most, since our estrangement, he would make a few cutting remarks from time to time, but nothing of consequence.

So I kept my composure, and my mother, serene, applauded: "Your brother is right, you will waste your time to no avail."

"The thing is, I've already found an apartment . . . "

Without warning, or even taking into account the presence of her son-in-law, who was an outsider, my mother the civilized woman, just like the grandmother in my memories, began to beat her breast.

"Oh, my God!" she cried out, in Arabic, "Are you really going to leave me?"

"It's a very nice big two-room apartment, just a few minutes from my work . . . "

"I don't want to know!" she shrieked, slapping each of her cheeks with such violence that she knocked her headscarf off.

Then, forcibly regaining her calm, wrapping her hair up again—it was long and wavy, gray, almost white—she murmured in French, "You didn't say a word, during the entire meal, and when finally you open your mouth it's to break my heart."

"Ali isn't very talkative either," said my sister.

"Ali is my son-in-law and he is our guest. I am talking about my son, the flesh of my flesh, and his behavior toward the woman who gave birth to him and sacrificed her life for him."

Turning to address her son-in-law, who sat so rigidly that you began to wonder whether this graduate from the prestigious political science institute wasn't a bit thick, she cranked up the refrain that was the story of her life.

"I may not look it, Ali my son, with my dresses and scarves and shut in all day long in this low-income housing unit, washing and mending and ironing and cleaning and cooking, but I was educated at the best girls' school in Blida. And in addition to my knowledge of theology and my passion for Arabic poetry, I was good at everything, above all literature. I read Colette and George Sand, Pierre Loti and André Gide, Victor Hugo and Lamartine, and many others. I had every chance of getting my baccalaureate and becoming an educated, independent woman, like so many of my old classmates who are now secondary school teachers at the very least. And, can you imagine, Ali my son, there is a member of the Académie Française who went to that very lycée. Yes, Ali my son."

Alain, also known as Ali, who had already had his share of his mother-in-law's reminiscing, was full of love for his wife, and listened to my mother with a display of unflagging interest.

"But fate decided otherwise," continued my mother. "I married, in keeping with my father's wishes, may God receive him in his Paradise, two summers before I would have graduated, and I have had no other occupation in life than to raise and educate my children with respect for their religion and their family."

Ordinarily, my mother's reminiscing stopped there. But that day, in honor of the announcement of my departure, she added, "My husband, who was also my cousin, an orphan whom my father had taken in, was already old, thirty-two years, and I was barely half his age, and he had very little education. But his wisdom and honesty were unequalled. A wisdom which, in the end, only Mahmoud has inherited—and Ourida, of course, my youngest who, praise be to God, has brought you, Ali my son, to our noble religion. Whereas Mohamed, my adored eldest, for whose sake I have bled myself dry, for whom I, the daughter of the master the entire city bowed down to, have ruined my eyes and broken my back, bending over a sewing machine, yet I would have done even more for him, even housecleaning, if I had not promised my late husband that I would never work outside the home, and now my son who has never ever been denied a single thing ends up going to live like a *kafir* in Paris."

"Ali and I live in Paris," my sister pointed out, in her calm voice.

"Ali was born in Paris," said my mother, irritably. "Mohamed was born in Blida, and he was raised by my late lamented father, and he grew up in Saint-Ouen, in this apartment. His life, his real life, has always been by his mother's side. And if he followed our customs to the letter, because he is the eldest, even if he were married he would stay by my side. But it is Mahmoud, may Allah protect him, who has sacrificed himself so that he may find his family under his poor mother's roof."

"Provided Mohamed makes up his mind to get married," grumbled my brother in Arabic.

"Inshallah," I murmured.

"It is the duty of every good Muslim to procreate as quickly as possible," said my brother in French, in his professorial tone.

"Inshallah," I repeated.

"Not inshallah. Right away!" shouted my brother abruptly, no longer quite so high and mighty.

Then, going back and forth between the two languages:

"You have turned down every single girl our mother has found for you. Even the mayor's daughter does not seem to meet with your approval. Our poor mother finally agreed to let you find a suitable one yourself. And she is waiting. *We* are waiting. You have to decide, and you have to hurry up, old boy. No one in this house is here only to be at your disposal."

"You are under no obligation to wait for me," I said calmly.

"You would have your young brother get married before you do?" asked my mother, indignantly.

"*Mektoub*, mother . . ."

"*Mektoub*, you want everyone in Blida to talk?" she shouted in Arabic. "You want all of Saint-Ouen to go saying there's something wrong with my son?" she concluded with a sob.

"You're imagining things, mother dear. People have other things to think about than to—"

Her eyes rolled upward and, her throat tight, she interrupted, "And you just do exactly as you like."

"You should thank the Creator that he made you a boy," hissed my brother.

Then, in his professorial tone, "Do you know what the Prophet, peace be upon him, said about parents?"

I held my tongue and fumed with annoyance. I was the eldest, after all, I did not have to submit to my younger brother's whimsical changes of tone, nor to his explicit demands, I thought, while he blushed and grew nervous in the face of my silence.

"Of course you know," he said eventually. "But I will remind you all the same. He said, peace be upon him, *Unconditional obedience of one's parents.* And regarding the issue of who, between the mother and the father, one must obey first, He not only replied, peace be upon him, *Your mother, your mother, your mother, then your father,* he added, *Ajanatou tahta aqdami el-oumahate.* Believers. It goes without saying."

Then for the benefit of the neophyte, pontificating, he translated: "Paradise lies at the feet of your mothers . . . Literally, my brother . . . "

Radiant, my mother nodded approvingly at my brother's words, and the radio announced the imminence of the *Dhuhr* prayer. My brother got up and turned up the volume. After murmuring a *La-ilah-ila-allah-Mohammed-rasul-allah* full of emphasis, his voice more professorial than ever, certain that I would refuse to accompany them to the mosque, he turned to my brother-in-law: "Come, Ali, my brother, let us do our duty. May God in his mercifulness accept our prayers and forgive our sins. Inshallah."

"Inshallah," echoed Alain also known as Ali.

The two men then evoked the great blessing, one out loud, the other in a murmur, to which blessing we were still responding in unison when the front door slammed shut.

My mother, he said, or the voice in my right ear, I'm not sure which, then whispered to me, "It will be your fault if your brother doesn't become a father until he's retired."

As if to flee the discussion, my sister hastily cleared the table.

"Go first to fulfill your duty to the Creator, my child," said my mother. "The dishes can wait."

"I am indisposed, mother," murmured my sister as she took away the last glass of tea.

"You're not pregnant yet, my child?" said my mother.

Fed on Judeo-Christian taboos, with a poor knowledge of Arabic, and consequently unused to the sauciness of the sort of gossip that the women would exchange in the baths and court-yards of Blida, my sister blushed right to her ears and said, "Oh, mother, it's hardly been six weeks . . . "

"So? I was pregnant on the very first night," said my mother, not without a certain note of pride.

"Yes, mother dear . . . "

"If I'd had to wait for six weeks, the twins would never have been born," she added, giving me a sidelong glance.

"Yes, mother dear . . . " sighed my sister.

"God will see to it," concluded my mother with a little pout of disappointment.

"Inshallah," murmured my sister, before hurrying out of the room.

Instead of getting up and unrolling her prayer mat, my mother merely sang a few praises to God and his Prophet. Then, as if getting her bearings, she fell silent. Which could only mean she was making ready for a stormy discussion that would be endless and, above all, exhausting.

I clenched my teeth and my mother moved her lips: "Why have you turned out so different from each other, you and Mahmoud?"

"We are still the same, my mother."

"How long has it been since you've been to the mosque?"

"Faith lives in people's hearts, my mother . . . "

"We hardly see you pray at home, either," she continued. "And your brother is suffering, he used to admire you so much, and swore by everything you knew. You were the first one to nurture him with the *suras* and the Hadith. What has become of you, my son? I no longer recognize you. Is it your studies which have distanced you from me and from your fine upbringing? Did I do something wrong by sending you to the best schools in the country? Will I have to pay for it for the rest of my days? Look at your brother-in-law, he too has degrees from a major school, but since he entered our religion he never misses a single prayer. Even on Fridays, when he has the time, he meets up with your brother at the Great Mosque. And you, Mohamed, my son, my favorite, to whom I gave the most noble of names, why are you behaving like a non-believer?"

"I am still the same, my mother . . . "

"*Tabtab*," she exclaimed, stirring the air with her hand, which meant she was not about to be taken for a fool.

"I respect you, my mother . . . "

"By going to live like a *kafir* in Paris, my son?" she said, in Arabic.

"I just want to be close to work . . . "

"And far away from your mother. You haven't forgotten

why the Prophet, peace be upon him, evoked the mother three times, have you?"

"For the suffering which she endures . . . "

"Something which fathers have no idea about," she continued. "And without the blessing of their mother, children will know neither happiness on earth nor the heavenly paradise . . . "

"You will see me often, my mother. I will come to Saint-Ouen as often as possible. I have a hard job, you know. To hold up, I need energy, I need to be organized . . . and I need your blessing."

"Do you think I brought my sons into this world so this would be the result? So they would finish me off before my time? Is that what you want, apple of my eye? To kill me?"

Find my way out of the rubble.

Endure your jeremiads no longer.

Be rid of your begetter-of-sons demands.

I want to live.

Freely.

I was about to toss this into her face. But I didn't. Pointless to torment her. I would have all the time I needed, sitting at my computer, in the lovely bedroom with its alcoves, overlooking the foliage and the singing blackbird, to release my words and settle my accounts, with the help of poetry. At this point in time, I needed her blessing.

Bestowing upon her the smile that always got the better of her, causing her to melt like ice cream in the sun, I said, "I absolutely have to be in Paris."

As she did not budge, I pursued, gravely, "If I am to progress in my work."

"Your living here didn't stop you being promoted every year, and with your degrees you can work wherever you want."

"And I work in Paris."

She burst into tears.

"What have I done to you?"

By the fourth sob I was on my feet. I knelt beside her, took her hand, kissed it several times over—another gesture which never left her unmoved—and said, "I don't mean to make you unhappy, my mother. But I have made my decision, and there's no going back."

"And Ramadan?" she asked, with a start.

"What about Ramadan?"

She took offense: "What do you mean, my son, what about Ramadan? Have you gone so far as to forget Ramadan?"

And she moaned: "To think that you are the only one of my children who received a real religious education. Do you remember how, in Blida, your grandfather would puff out his chest when he went with you at dawn to the Koranic school?"

"I remember, my mother," I replied, scarcely able to hide my weariness.

"So how will you spend Ramadan, then, all alone in Paris?"

"It is only July, my mother, and this year Ramadan isn't until October . . . "

"September," she corrected.

"Between now and then—"

"Between now and then you will surely be married, my son," she interrupted, suddenly enthusiastic.

"That's right, my mother, between now and then I will surely be married," I sighed.

"And I'll be able to leave this world with my soul in peace."

"After a long life, my mother."

"Before Ramadan?"

"Yes, my mother . . . "

"You promise?"

"Inshallah, my mother. Before Ramadan."

"Inshallah, apple of my eye. And then your brother can get married in turn. Otherwise his fiancée's parents will end up giving their daughter to another family. And what would become of your brother?"

"That's true, my mother."

"And then we can make the *hajj* as planned. Your brother and his wife, and you and your wife, inshallah, *ya rabbi*. Ourida and Ali. All together, my son, to the holy places . . . "

"Yes, my mother."

"Maybe you already have someone in mind, my son?"

"I have no one in mind, my mother. For the time being."

"You came home late last night . . . "

"Work, my mother . . . So do I have your blessing?" I quickly asked.

"You do, apple of my eye, you do." She went, standing up straight and, reaching for her prayer mat, she murmured the ritual salutations.

Delighted that things had come to this positive conclusion, I got up and in turn unrolled a prayer mat next to my pious mother.

It wasn't all that complicated after all, scorpion, whispered the voice into my left ear just as my mother and I began our prostrations.

At the end of the afternoon, after numerous negotiations to be released from the obligation to stay for supper, with my suitcase and my old sleeping bag in the trunk, my new books and a few of my records on the passenger seat, and my computer and my little stereo on the backseat, I left the low-income-housing district of Saint-Ouen, pursued by packages of *makrouts*, and sobs, and my mother's reminders.

You'll eat them for breakfast, apple of my eye.

Find yourself a proper girl, my son.

Your choices will be mine, my adored one.

Don't forget your mother, light of my days.

And so on and so forth, until the car took off toward the lights of Paris.

PART TWO
THE LOST WOMEN

"There is no sure concomitance that is not
accompanied by a coincidence."
L'Intuition de l'instant
GASTON BACHELARD

"What stranger here does not feel at home?
But that is how you feel, as soon as night falls.
In this immense city, you do not have your place,
Or so you believe; the nightmare is beginning."
Ombre gardienne
MOHAMED DIB

A week later, said he, the night was at its peak, the city was bubbling with excitement, and I went back to my apartment, alone. I had just spent the evening with the forty-something woman, who simply dumped me right there outside the restaurant.

We had had dinner at the little Thai place on the rue Jules-Chaplain, two strides from my house. A dinner during which she began by describing in detail her former life in Algiers, where she used to teach, living with her family in the heart of the Kasbah—"I was free during the day, and locked up at night," she had said with a smile. Her mother, desperate over the fact that her daughter had no suitor, and certain that the girl was bewitched, had gone off searching for the swallow which, according to the matron of the house, carried the curse that was responsible for the spell cast over her daughter, she had added. But that was a long story.

Then all of a sudden, with none of the poise or restraint she had shown on our first meeting, she became completely hyper, borderline obscene, and poured out her feelings as if I were her lifelong friend. Something one ought never to do in the presence of a future and imminent lover.

In the beginning, with the exception of a few passages which she related without blushing or batting an eyelash—for example, that in Algiers, to get her passport, she had had to sleep with an important civil servant, an execrable but power-ful guy—I was hoping that she would soon cease spilling out her sordid past, for my mind was focused rather on my leather sofa and my single malt scotch and my oval bathtub and the blackbird's song, and I was looking forward to the steamy night that awaited me, or so I thought, and so I confess I did not retain much of what she was telling me.

Then, fearful she might become aware of my lack of interest, I forced myself to follow her tale, which I picked up again at the point when she was describing how she went through hell to sort out her situation—immigrant shelters, soup kitchens, suicide attempts, psychoanalysts from the Primo Levi Association, or something like that, without whom, she whispered, she would not be here calmly having dinner with me. Then more sleeping around to help with the paperwork, to make it official. With a socialist member of parliament. A nice enough guy, she said, but he was getting old, and sticky.

When I nearly choked on a mouthful of Pad Thai she finally changed the subject, and informed me that she had read *Djamila and Her Mother* (the book she'd been leafing through at the Flore, and which, she reminded me, had attracted my attention) and that she knew the author personally. They'd met in Algiers. In the literature department at the university. And in Paris the novelist had put her up for a time, which enabled her to stop her drifting, and the novelist had helped her with formalities and all that. When her first novel came out, my forty-something was still living under her roof, but because of a journalist who had revealed that the author was using a pseudonym, insinuating moreover that she would never write another book, Loubna Minbar had sunk into paranoia worthy of psychiatric confinement—she saw killers everywhere, a man in a raincoat outside her window, another one who was stalking her all over Paris— and no longer opened the door or even the shutters, she never left the house, not even to go to work, so she lost the job that she'd had in addition to the freelance stuff she did here and there for the papers and which she signed under her own name and which had enabled her to pay for her room and board. And then, when she learned that a certain historian who specialized in Algeria had been obliged to accept a position in Vietnam following threats he'd received, she left Paris nearly crazy with panic and went into exile elsewhere—Sidi Bou Said, Berlin, Zurich, Hamburg—and as a result my interlocutor, Hadda Bouchnaffa, once again found herself out in the street.

Thinking about my project for a book, but without mentioning it to her, I asked her if she could give me her friend's contact information. But she refused, under the pretext that her novelist friend had shut herself away so that she could write, and that she traveled a great deal, not to run away, but because her books were published in a number of countries and, in any case, not a single one of her friends was seeing her these days. And that when it was all over, she moved on.

"When it was all over?"

Sidestepping my question, she began to talk about the novelist again who, it would seem, was at that very moment, while we were conversing, working on some sort of interview with an Islamist whose mother, a widow of fifty years old or so and who used to be pious and a real stickler for principles, had virtually converted overnight to sin and was living with a poet, a West Indian who was not only as black as coal but also Christian to the tips of his fingers. Yes. Yes. And that through this story Loubna Minbar revealed episodes of her own life, like the one about the journalist-informer with his crummy reviews, or the one about the Algerian novelist who, because she had criticized him for taking everybody in with his female pseudonym and his crime fiction, had nicknamed her Madame Alas. Or the story about the director of the Algerian Cultural Center who, because her books did not flatter his country's politics, was so hostile that he refused to send her invitations for any of the Center's events. And a few more anecdotes of that nature—spite, revenge, censorship, and so on.

Whatever the case may be, she said, Loubna Minbar, who now lived among the Bohemian chic and the gauche caviar, had changed. She avoided her own sisters, forgot her father's existence, and, above all, looked down on her fellow creatures, only agreeing to meet with them in order to advance her literary projects. Like that poor guy who'd gone off to Greenland, and had spent his time, compass in hand, trying to determine which way was Mecca. Like that poor girl—tossed back and forth between the demands of her mother, who was crazy, and those of a country that was going down the tubes—who from one day to the next had proclaimed herself to be *The Sultana of the Kasbah*. Or the young girl stricken with amnesia whom you could read about in *The Kidnapper in the House Across the Street*. Or the one with a crippled toe, in *The Time of Punishments*. Or the one whose pubic hair was white as snow, in *Djamila and her Mother*. Had I read any of those books? she asked suddenly.

"Which books?"

"Well, the ones by you-know-who . . . Loubna Minbar . . . "

"Uh . . . no," I said.

"In any case," she continued. "Anyone who goes near that woman—she steals people's lives—inevitably ends up losing their mind. Just reading her is enough to send you round the bend."

"Oh, really?"

"Yes," she said, nodding, gravely raising an eyebrow as if to reinforce the veracity of her words.

And, she had concluded, she was in a good position to know . . .

As I was certain she didn't know you from Adam, and that I was dealing with an expert compulsive liar, to be honest, I really couldn't care less what sort of mental state she was in; my prevailing interest was to drag her off to my little Versailles and peel off the layers on top of the string that you could see sticking out of her trousers. So I insisted upon the fact that it really didn't matter to me to meet her *friend*, and I began to ask her questions about her life. At present . . .

Cheerful and obliging straight off the bat, she informed me that she lived in the 20th arrondissement, on rue de Ménil-montant, in a fairly spacious apartment on the sixth floor; there was an elevator, but the apartment faced north, and was so dark that she had to have the light on all the time, and above all it cost an arm and a leg, but she shared it, fortunately, with two colleagues from the publishing house where for the last five years she had been in charge of final edits on manuscripts. One of her colleagues was going to throw a big party for her for her fourtieth birthday, and she would invite me. If I wanted her to.

I did not, obviously, but I said, "Please," and she said, "Good, good," and then she started on her communal living arrangements, how the chores were divided up, little dinner parties among friends, and so on.

Addled by the wine, annoyed, I was no longer listening. I was struggling against the urge to grab hold of her and drag her to the very place where I had been intending to drag her all along, and I let my brain go into over-drive:

Why must you wait for your girlfriend's party, my lovely? And if your insalubrious and overpopulated abode will not do, I shall cordially invite you to my own, which is hardly a dump, but rather a nest where you will be cosseted like a precious tropical bird. An aging tropical bird, to be sure, but one who leaves no doubts as to her erotic potential. You shall drink my scotch, you shall waddle among my furnishings and my mag-nificent ceiling, you shall gaze at your reflection in my authen-tic period mirrors and in the mother-of-pearl of my eyes, you will splash about in the oval bathtub and between my virile legs, you will roll on my carpets and on my perfumed skin, we shall rumple and soak the satin sheets . . . My priceless satin sheets. An arm and a leg. A small fortune.

She talked about her roommates—one was Chilean, the other Cuban, both refugees, and like her they'd had a rough time of it, they were survivors, damaged but full of life and talent, who scouted for Hispanic authors or something like that. I couldn't take it any more so I downed my digestif in one and asked her if they were pretty.

"Who, pretty?" she said.

"Your roommates," I replied indolently, one eye glued to the naked woman at the bottom of my little saké cup.

For a moment her gaze once again took on that hard and frightened expression. And then, serenely, a bit royally even, she took a big gulp of wine and lit a cigarette.

She blew the smoke sideways and raised an eyebrow, and her expression seemed to say that here was a guy who did not deserve her company, a guy who was insane, unhinged, a pervert . . .

No, mademoiselle, I am not insane, I am a virgin who has had enough, and I am inviting you to offer me your pussy, because, young-woman-who-is-close-to-my-mother's-age, while I do know more or less what that creature looks like (how often had I spent my lunch hour hanging out at the Musée d'Orsay to gaze at the dominant red tones of Courbet's *L'Origine du monde*), I know nothing about its odor or its texture. And you, young-woman-who-is-forty-four-years-old-who-could-be-the-mother-of-my-little-sister, what color is your fleece? as black as your smoldering irises? or already made hoary by time and the ageing pricks you have received therein?

And so on with my rambling until silence reached a peak. Fearing that she might simply end the evening, I set out to repair my blunder.

"I just wanted to know whether your roommates are as pretty as you are," I said, smiling to the full extent of my very white teeth.

Shrugging her shoulders with disdain, she stubbed out her cigarette and poured herself another glass of wine.

"You are very pretty, you know," I ventured.

"Thank you," she said, without the slightest emotion.

"And you?"

"Me?"

"What do you think of me?"

She raised both eyebrows.

"I mean, physically, and all . . . "

"Fine," she began, somewhat addled by my question, as if she had no clue as to my motivations, as if I had invited her there for no other purpose than to hear her reel off all her insane nonsense.

"Fine, in what way?" I insisted.

"Fine . . . Perfectly fine."

"And?"

"You are a regular sultan," she said, without a moment's hesitation, taking in my Ralph Lauren shirt, and the Montblanc pen that was peeking conspicuously out of the shirt pocket.

"Thank you," I said, proud as a peacock, at that point far from suspecting anything that might remotely have resembled an allusion or a touch of irony on her part, still less a premonition.

And what if this were a head-on attack on your part?

"So, why don't we become lovers?" I added right away, lightly and discreetly touching my left ear, staring at the wrinkle that cut subtly across her forehead.

"You've had a bit to drink," she said, with icy indulgence.

"I'm serious," I persisted.

At which point she laughed, gently, with that same indulgence. And then, utterly unexpectedly, she placed her hand on my arm. Convinced that she was accepting my proposition at last, that she would go with me right there and then to my quarters, I began chomping at the bit: "Fine. I'll get the check and let's get out of here."

"I'm already with someone," she said, withdrawing her hand.

"I'm sure you are," I retorted. "Even if you had children and in-laws and cousins and an entire tribe—"

"Nothing like that," she interrupted.

"Fine, fine," I said again, chomping some more at the bit and waving to the waiter. "Let me pay and we can go."

She smiled, almost tenderly.

"Listen, Mohamed, I just told you, I'm with someone . . . "

"Frankly, that doesn't bother me," I said.

"Well it bothers me," she said sharply, crushing her cigarette.

Sensing defeat, imagining my empty-handed return to my luxurious apartment, I was about to resign myself and leave this sicko behind, but I told her to think about my proposition. She poured some more wine and said, "Okay."

She's flattered, I thought. Forty-four years old, a woman can be nothing but flattered by so much solicitude. And she must be making a list of all my qualities. Young. Single. Cultured. Enviable professional status. A fine address. Physique not bad, not bad at all, and I had neither bad breath nor smelly feet, and in fact I had just come from the *hammam* at Barbès, where I'd let myself be royally pampered, massaged, and exfoliated, and I'd had my pubic hair trimmed, my nails filed, and my armpits perfumed. That's what my father used to do when he had his paid leave. That's what any good Muslim will do before copulating.

In any event, Arabs like me are in short supply on the streets of Saint-Germain. And I knew, or at least I thought I knew, through my cousin in particular, that Algerian women, of whatever stripe, educated or illiterate, from a comfortable or modest milieu, born in Constantine or Amiens or Malibu, aspired to only one thing: to hook up with an Algerian man. No long-winded negotiations regarding conversion. No need to Islamicize the name. No circumcision. So the "emancipated women" came looking for us, if not among the epicureans, at least among the non-practicing.

Was I not, now, one of them? Moreover, I wasn't asking for the moon, in the name of a life of *babasse*.[1] Just a few nights. One night. Had she not offered herself when she was young and surely prettier than she was now at the age of forty to men who were repulsive to her?

Her mind suddenly elsewhere, as if she were in a hurry to leave the place, to leave me, basically, she again blew her cigarette smoke to one side and looked at her watch.

"It's getting late," she murmured, just as the waiter was putting the check on the table.

And she wished to contribute to her share of said check. Given the defeat I was about to suffer, I could have let her go ahead. But as a gentleman through and through, and one who wished he could keep her for the night—above all, perhaps, I had hoped she would at least agree to a nightcap at my place—I raised my hand ostentatiously and said, "It's out of the question."

And paid for the lot with my American Express.

Outside the restaurant, my invitation for a "nightcap" was irremediably declined, and she thanked me for dinner, then placed a kiss on my cheek. One kiss. One alone. A sign, I thought, of encouragement, that next time, maybe tomorrow, since Monday was my day off, and the publishing house where she worked was in the neighborhood, after a nice boozy lunch, she would end up in my bed. Until the early morning.

"And tomorrow?"

"What about tomorrow?"

"We could have lunch . . . "

---

[1] An abbot or a priest, pejorative word used to describe an old bachelor (Mohamed).

"Call me," she said, hailing a taxi with the ease of the true Parisian woman.

"I don't have your number," I said.

"Here," she said, handing me a business card.

Then she got into the taxi and waved.

She's flattered, I thought again, watching the taxi pull away.

She's flattered, I could not stop thinking, as I closed the door to my apartment. Flattered, but the fact remained: I had come home alone.

My first weekend as a free man, he said, and I had come home alone. Like a condemned man. How would I make it through the night? No television. No girly magazines to consult. Not even anyone across the way, some silhouette in the night to keep me company. As for writing, my soaked brain would not last a single line. What if I called her on her cell phone? I would excuse myself profusely for my lack of tact, and renew my invitation. Maybe this time she'd relent? Maybe I had just not insisted hard enough, and she was afraid of being taken for an easy lay? That must be it, I thought. She didn't want me to think she was fast.

So I put on my slippers, and opened my cell phone, ready to call her. If I insisted too much, however, it could compromise our next meeting. And this forty-something was all I had to nibble on, so to speak, because, although it may have been summer, my work at the bank was piling up, I had files to catch up on, and the intern, ugly as a louse—how in this day of lasers and contact lenses can anyone still have bifocal glasses?—was about as efficient as a twit. In short, I did not know any other women, and given the endless stacks of toil ahead, I would not know any other women until my vacation, scheduled for winter, during which, as I promised my mother, I would be somewhere between Mecca and Medina. Pilgrimage, I thought, rubbing my hands, during which I would have ample opportunity to expiate my upcoming infallible fornication.

For I was certain that the forty-something would fall into my arms. As of the very next day. Call me, she had said, as she was hailing her taxi.

In practice, I knew nothing about women. That is true. But in theory, I knew more than enough to suspect that she had acted cold all the better to give herself to me, warmed to perfection, when the time came. Could it be, too, that she had never suspected a cool dude like myself would court her, so she had neglected to wax? or she had her period? or maybe she was simply someone whose maxim in life was "slowly but surely"? Translation: a good fuck, all in good time. She'd methodically gone about getting her passport, in Algiers, and then her papers in Paris, and now she was planning to end her career as an old maid in exile without a family. Was I not the ideal candidate? The sultan of Saint-Germain? An excellent party, who would give her nothing to be ashamed of?

Thus, I gave up on the idea of calling her, and once again regretted the absence of a television. All that was left to do was inaugurate the bottle of single malt. Alone. I switched on my factory-style lamp, then lit the candle with its whiff of musk, the one I had set by the fireplace in anticipation of the evening, along with the dozen or so little candles all around the bathtub. But they would be for another time. Call me, she had said, hailing her taxi.

After I had put on a CD, Brahms's fourth symphony—also premeditated—I opened the bottle of scotch and breathed in the aroma of leather and peat. That forty-something seemed to like her booze and, despite her age and the hard times she'd been through, she could hold it well. She would have liked this scotch. But she'd run away.

As I took my first swallow, the flashing light on the answering machine caught my eye. And what if, while I was on my way home, she had phoned to tell me she'd come for that nightcap after all?

I swallowed the scotch down in one gulp, lit a cigarette, and listened to the calls. Five, all from my mother, and I erased them right away. I sank deep into my leather sofa, with my feet on the coffee table, poured another glass, and meditated upon the present moment, inclined to savor it just as I intended to savor this second glass.

Then I heard the iron curtain of the brasserie coming down, which told me that it was two o'clock in the morning, and that millions of men and women on the planet were swapping their saliva, their secretions. Whereas I was high and dry. In this labyrinth of boredom. No television. No slits or clefts or odors or sweat, I ruminated, cursing the old lady right back to her first ancestor.

I poured some more to drink, crumpled the empty pack of cigarettes and opened another. As I was clicking the lighter I thought that a call girl could get me out of all this. Out of solitude and out of abstinence. That the forty-something from the Kasbah could go to hell with her roommates and her "I'm with someone." A little surf on the Internet and no sooner said than done.

But how much would it cost me, I wondered, switching on the computer. I'm not stingy, but still. I had just maxed out my American Express card at the Thai restaurant; Mademoiselle Bouchnaffa had chosen the wine; her expensive tastes had shot up the total on the check and, of course, two whole bottles had ended up in our glasses. In hers, above all. Drunk to the dregs.

I gave up on the call girl idea and ordered a few books through my usual provider. I switched the machine off and took the few steps back into my lovely living room. I swept the room with my gaze, appreciating my furniture, the way I'd arranged things, the fireplace, the French doors that opened out onto the balcony. Mademoiselle Papinot would be really impressed by my expensive taste . . .

And what if I called her? I could use a sudden decision to

buy an apartment as a pretext. In the 20th or the 18th arrondissement. I could say that such a decision warranted our meeting within the hour. She would climb out of her warm sheets and call a taxi, which I would pay for. I would wait for her downstairs, I'd open the front door to her, she'd be scantily dressed, perhaps even stark naked beneath a raincoat, she would reveal all her finery to me, in the elevator, I would promise her a fur coat, for winter, and a vacation in Chamonix. All pie in the sky. It goes without saying. But none the less persuasive. That too goes without saying.

And so on and so forth with all a novice's vague desires, until my brain grew quite soft and the bottle was empty. Then I took a Stilnox and went into the bedroom, taking my cell phone with me, just in case Hadda Bouchnaffa, filled with remorse or overcome with a sudden desire to get it off, decided to call me.

Naked as a worm, a luxury I could at last indulge in, I slipped under the comforter and promised myself I would commit no more blunders.

Are they pretty? I heard myself say, just as I was drifting into a sleep as deep as death.

I was dreaming of three brunettes, he said, with round, firm, quivering breasts, when the ringing of the phone woke me up.

I switched on the night light and read the name on the screen.

"Good morning, my mother . . . "

"How did you know it was me?"

"It says so on the screen, my mother . . . "

"But I'm not calling you on your cell phone."

"But it says so on the landline, too . . . "

"Aren't you up yet, apple of my eye?"

"I went to bed late. An urgent file . . . "

"These nights of staying up late are going to wear you out."

"Yes, my mother."

I looked at my watch. It wasn't even nine o'clock.

"It's Sunday, my mother, and at this time of day, the entire city is asleep."

"I won't bother you much longer, my son, but I hope you haven't forgotten that you're having lunch at home? Your brother-in-law and sister will be here . . . "

Of course I had forgotten. Not only had I forgotten, but I had planned on spending the entire day in bed. With the forty-something. Who had run away.

"No, my mother, I hadn't forgotten."

"I called you over four times to remind you. You never pick up the phone."

"I stayed in my office."

"Your cell phone was switched off."

"I had a lot of work . . . "

"May God assist you, my son. But try to be on time for lunch. Your brother went to do the shopping. By metro, the poor boy. I hope he won't be late. We had all been counting on you to do the shopping. It's so much easier with the car. I asked you to in one of my messages."

I yawned audibly.

"So you don't listen to your messages?"

"I got home late, my mother."

"I'll be off now, but please be on time, apple of my eye."

"Yes, my mother."

I crawled out of bed and went into the living room. I swallowed a shot of whisky, just so as to pick up my dream where I'd left off, and I went back into the bedroom. After I'd unplugged the land line and turned off the cell, I burrowed under the comforter.

When I awoke it was nearly two in the afternoon. My brother and brother-in-law must be at the mosque, and my mother must be cursing me.

Shit, I swore.

I took a shower, drank a first coffee, then another one, and took the third one into my study. For a long time I gazed at the trembling foliage. Then I called the forty-something. I suggested lunch at the Flore. She told me once again that the Café de Flore was a bit too "white" for her, and added that she preferred the bistros in Ménilmontant where, she simpered, she could feel like the sultana of the Kasbah all over again.

"Fair enough," I said. "Let's have lunch in Ménilmontant."

But she turned down my invitation outright. And when I insisted, she murmured that she was not alone.

"Bring him along," I said casually.

Upon which, laughing a little, she retorted that Hadda

Bouchnaffa was open-minded but not a complete idiot, old boy. And besides, "he is a she," she pointed out. Sorry, sorry, I said. Don't worry about it, she said, adding that she'd call me soon.

"You're not mad at me, then?"

"Not at all. Talk to you soon, Mohamed."

Why hadn't she mentioned her sexual deviancy to me? Surely I did not bear the marks of some old-fashioned bigot. My manner of expressing myself may have been somewhat prudish, that is true, but my advances could hardly have been more explicit. Moreover, her venal copulating, at least the way she had explained it to me, did not seem to cause her any qualms.

Well, so what. The next time she called, I would also invite her girlfriend. Straight to my house. And why not. Champagne, expensive wine, candles, caterer, that perfect Parisian woman, flawless example of French and republican integration, could hardly refuse such gallantry . . . So I would go from one to the other, drinking and inhaling their secretions, sweet-smelling as musk, rich as honey.

Well, so what, I thought again, my spirits high.

I got dressed and went out, curious and happy to be exploring my neighborhood on a summer Sunday. The brasserie opposite my building was closed. As was the one on the corner of the rue du Regard and boulevard Raspail.

I was idling along the boulevard, through the stalls of the organic market, the most expensive one in France, I've heard, which was closing up, when I noticed Nawar and his wife with their dog in tow. I waved to him but, admonishing his dog— Come here, Jugurtha[1]—my friend looked away.

Continuing on my way, I spotted a bistro that wasn't much to look at, but at least it was open. As I drew nearer, I was able to

---

[1] King of Numidia, also the name of the dog belonging to former president Valéry Giscard d'Estaing (Mohamed).

read the menu displayed outside. Couscous-Royal. Couscous-lamb. Couscous-merguez. Couscous-chicken. And so on.

Integration in reverse, I thought, convinced the proprietor must be white.

I was about to go in when I caught a glimpse of the proprietor's face. Instantly recalling something I had read in *Buried Alive*,[1] I hightailed it out of there. A few minutes later, I was outside the Café de Flore.

I went into the café, and I saw her right away. Twenty-something, dark, almost black skin, large dark eyes, long wavy hair, she was sipping eagerly on a Perrier with mint syrup. Her gaze, hard and frightened at the same time, met mine. And as if by magic, before I even sat down, she responded to my smile.

---

[1] "[. . .] if I was dead, they would take me to the mosque in Paris and I would find myself in the hands of filthy Arabs; so I would die twice over, they make me sick!" Sadeq Hedayat (Mohamed).

The sky was ablaze with Bastille Day fireworks, he said, when I closed the door to my lovely nest. I was alone, yet again, but just before she got out of the car, she brushed her lips against mine. I repeat, out loud, and out of order: against mine her lips she brushed. And again. With her sweet lips did the very young woman brush my own.

A chaste kiss, to be sure, but a good beginning.

Before taking her home, I had suggested continuing the evening in a bar on the boulevard Montparnasse or in Saint-Germain, at the jazz club right near the Flore, where we had dined, drinking Perrier water—because she did not touch a drop of alcohol, and was respecting Ramadan, not out of tra-dition, she explained, but out of conviction, do you under-stand? She was worthy of her name, Khadija, that of the Prophet's first wife, who knew neither concubines nor co-wives, who believed with unflinching determination in the Messenger of God who had supported him and looked after him when, returning from Mount Hira, he was shivering with fever, overwhelmed by the apparitions of Jibril and the divine revelations that the Archangel with six hundred wings had made to him. She also said that my parents had given me the finest of names, and, if I didn't mind, she would refrain from calling me "Momo."

I approved, and she insisted that she could not stay, that I must not break my promise to take her home in due course, her sister-in-law would not like it if I did—for she lived with her sister-in-law, her brother's widow, on rue de la Pompe in the 16th arrondissement, and she had only granted her permission to stay out until eleven o'clock, and if she were late that could put an end to any other evening dates, she said.

Because, she added, if her father, who was upright and strict, were to find out that she was going out in the evening, he would put an end to her studies—she was a student in astrophysics—and repatriate her without delay, for her father, along with her mother and sisters, who had been refugees in France once upon a time, had since gone back to Algeria, she said. And it was a long story.

So her father would not like it at all if he were to find out that his twenty-five-year-old daughter was hanging around the dark streets of Paris. Bastille Day or no Bastille Day. But her sister-in-law, a musician, was young and modern, and had agreed to cover for her. Exceptionally. Because, she told me, she was a serious girl, and she only cared about her studies, and then, just like that, between two sips of Perrier, she told me that she would soon be moving to my neighborhood, to the rue Notre-Dame-des-Champs, so that she would be closer to her school. A little two-room apartment that her father had paid cash for, and she would be living there alone, like a big girl, cozy as could be.

Because, she said, her father would do anything to make sure his eldest daughter had all the comfort she deserved, and that her very trying studies deserved. Because she was a serious girl, she said again, worthy of the education her father was providing for her. She wasn't one of those girls who only thought about fun. And in a week, at the latest, once the work on the apartment was finished, she would no longer be under her sister-in-law's surveillance; thus, she would stop calling every twenty minutes, she said with a smile, picking up her vibrating cell phone.

After she had hung up she stared right at me and asked me

if I knew that Venus was a real mystery, an inhospitable planet, completely veiled and sculpted by volcanoes. And that it blazed away at 480 degrees Celsius, even though the sun had never penetrated its sky. And that it orbited backward. And maybe that was where infidels went to roast, she continued, picking up her cell phone, which had started vibrating again.

"It's my sister-in-law again," she said, before answering.

Sister-in-law or no sister-in-law, this was my second date as a free man and I was still a virgin. All I had to pass the time was my television, which I had finally bought and had delivered the day before.

After I pressed the button on the remote control, I inaugurated a new bottle of scotch. I lit a cigarette and checked my phone messages. Five and all from my mother, and I erased them immediately. I poured a glass and took little sips, thinking about the place where, next Saturday, I would take my girlfriend. Because, I said to myself again, that's what she was. She was my girlfriend. My first real girlfriend. The one I'd go to restaurants with, and the cinema, every Saturday, with or without the approval of her sister-in-law—that modern woman who, before granting permission to her protégée to stay out until eleven, had insisted upon speaking to me on the phone, and asking me about my person, and about the place where I planned to take her little sister-in-law, and above all extracting a promise from me that I'd make sure her young protégée got home. On time, please. Her father, you see, could call at any time. You're Algerian, aren't you? So you know the tune . . . And besides, she added, her father, who wasn't actually her father but her mother's husband, a well-known playwright in Algeria, was as fond of Samira as of the apple of his eye.

"Khadija," I corrected.

"I'm Khadija, Samira borrowed that name for her new life. A way of thanking me. It's true she really had a rough time of it, poor kid, the way only a slave can have a rough time of it. But all that is behind her now. I'm counting on you, all right?"

"Yes," I said, flattered by the trust placed in me by the sister-in-law of my young thing.

My steady girlfriend, whom I would not introduce to my (future) friends, only to my cousin. In any case, I didn't count on staying with her for all eternity. Just long enough to possess her. Maybe the atmosphere of a party might prove propitious? Driss, back in Paris, was planning to host one, and had cordially invited me. I would talk it over with my nymphet, my gazelle, my Turkish delight.

Or on the other hand, maybe I should simply surprise her with dinner at home? Tablecloth and candles. Caterer. Quiet music. Callas or Léo Ferré. Never out of fashion. Or Gaâda Diwane de Béchar, whom she'd listened to over and over in my old Peugeot.

After the fourth scotch, the idea of having dinner at home didn't seem like such a good one, dangerous at the very least. She would take it badly and I'd never see her again.

Above all you mustn't lose her, whispered the voice into my right ear.

Of course not, I murmured.

Your mother would like her, whispered the voice again into my right ear.

When I leapt up, the glass went flying and the scotch splattered all over the sofa.

She won't get away with it, I said to myself as I headed for the kitchen.

The she-wolf had to give up her role as guardian and master. Let her marry off the devout son and leave you alone, whispered the voice, finally, into my left ear.

Right. Damn right, I murmured, sponging off the sofa.

But what's this then—you're consorting with a girl you can scarcely tell apart from the mayor's daughter, the sort of girl your mother would welcome with ululations fit to rip her glottis out, whispered the voice again into my left ear.

Right. Damn right, I murmured, heading back to the kitchen.

Back in the living room I lit a cigarette and took a swig of scotch straight from the bottle.

Ululations fit to bleed her tonsils out, whispered the voice into my left ear.

No fear, I said out loud. My mother will not put the noose around my neck. Nor will she put it around the neck of that daddy's girl, whose daddy isn't her daddy, and from whom I expect only one thing. After that she can go to the devil, and as for me, with the newfound confidence conferred by my deflowering, I shall go to other women as white and free as a summer's breeze, I murmured, swallowing my Stilnox.

I took my cell phone, in case she called to thank me for the nice evening and wish me a good and pleasant night, and I went into the bedroom.

I got undressed and slipped under the comforter. A moment later, I fell into a sleep as deep as death.

I was dreaming of a young woman all of gold and silk attired, he said, and a thundering chorus of ululations was bursting my eardrums, when the ringing of the telephone woke me up.

"Good morning, my mother . . . "

"How do you know it's me?"

"Because I can see it on the screen, my mother, I told you already . . . "

"Aren't you up yet, apple of my eye?"

"I went to bed late . . . "

"Staying up so late all the time . . . "

"It was Bastille Day, my mother . . . "

"Exactly, and today is Friday. Your sister and brother-in-law, and your brother's fiancée and her family are coming to lunch, and we will all go together to hear the *khutab*. It's so rare."

"Yes, my mother."

"You should get here before the others do. It would look unseemly if my eldest son is not here to greet his brother-in-law and his future sister-in-law's family."

"Yes, my mother."

"Don't go performing your trick of not showing up. Last time we waited over an hour before we started eating. No way to get hold of you. This mania of yours, always switching off your phone, my son . . . So it was your brother, once again, who had to go do the shopping. On the metro, can you imagine what a chore that is? I'm expecting him, and I hope he won't be late."

"I'm going to give him my car. In a week at the latest."

"And what about you, my pet?"

"I'll buy another one."

"Keep your money, my son."

"I have to buy a new one for my business trips outside Paris."

"If next Sunday you could take care of the shopping, my pet . . . Why don't you come on Saturday? Your bed is where it's always been, my pet . . . "

"It depends whether I have work or not . . . "

"You can't have work every Saturday!"

"I am running four branches at once, my mother, and I have over four hundred people working for me. And banks, as you know, are open on Saturday, and, as the boss, I am supposed to stay in the office until morning, if need be. Moreover, I'm hoping for a promotion, and if I want to be sure of getting one, I have to work hard, my mother."

"I know, my son, but don't forget to come, apple of my eye."

"Yes, my mother."

I crawled out of bed and went into the living room. I swallowed a shot of whisky, to help me get back to sleep that much easier, and I went back into the bedroom. After I'd unplugged the land line and switched off the cell phone, I burrowed under the comforter.

When I woke up it was well past three o'clock in the afternoon. The *khutab* must be over by now, and your mother must be cursing you, whispered the voice in my right ear.

Shit, I swore.

I had a shower, and drank a coffee, and called my young thing. I suggested we have lunch at the Flore. She accepted eagerly.

The following Sunday, he said, I was dreaming about a virgin dressed in pink when the telephone awoke me. As I was picking up the receiver, I could feel her moving, rubbing against me.

Yes indeed. She is here. In my bed. Between my sheets. She had refused to go with me to Driss's party, she didn't like that sort of thing, parties, you never knew who would be there, and Driss, whom we'd run into at the Flore, did not seem trustworthy to her, she confessed, but she agreed to come to dinner . . . at my house. Because you know how to cook? she had asked, by way of consent.

"Good morning, my mother."

"Why are you whispering?"

"Because of the cat, my mother."

"You have a cat now?"

"Yes, my mother. Well, it's only temporary, I'm looking after him for my neighbors while they're on vacation."

"And since when do you have to whisper around cats?"

"It's a pedigreed cat, my mother, and it's very sensitive to noise."

She moved again and, like a feline, jumped out of the bed. In her pink cotton pajamas, she rushed into the bathroom.

I was resisting the onslaught of my mother's words when, wrapped in a towel, her hair wet, she reappeared. I tried to motion to her but, turning her back to me, without dropping her towel and with a magician's speed and agility, she managed to get dressed without allowing a single morsel of skin to fall prey to my avaricious eyes.

Then, as if she had the devil at her heels, she left the bedroom. I heard her in the kitchen using the coffee machine.

"Excuse me, my mother, I have to hang up."

"Not until you hear what I have to say."

"Hold the line, my mother, the cat is sneaking out the door."

The moment I jumped out of bed I heard the front door slam. I picked up the receiver.

"He got away, my mother. The cat got away," I said, making no effort to restrain a hiccup that was very close to a sob.

"Go get him, but don't forget to come, apple of my eye. I miss you, light of my days."

With my gaze focused on the unopened packet of condoms, I hung up. She had hardly even grazed my lips with her own when we lay down. What was her excuse? She had none. She confirmed that she was a virgin. Her studies came first, she added. And I will ask you to keep your underwear on, she had commanded, in Arabic, while her cell phone was vibrating. It's my sister-in-law, she said, refusing the call.

"Why don't you answer?" I asked.

"I don't live at her place anymore and she's getting on my nerves," she replied, slipping under the covers.

And what if the calls were not from her sister-in-law at all but from a lover? A female lover? What did I know? My patience was wearing thin, but there was no end to the surprises in store. And I was still as chaste as a parish priest.

I dialed her number.

"Where are you?" I asked, a tad authoritarian.

"On the rue Notre-Dame-des-Champs, almost outside my house," she replied nonchalantly.

Softening my tone I said, "Shall we have lunch together?"

"I'd love to but I'm expecting my sister-in-law. She's taking me to IKEA, I need some bookshelves."

"I would have taken you there if you'd asked."

"Some other time."

"I can help you put up the bookshelves . . . "

"No, thanks. We'll manage."

"I hope that call from my mother had nothing to do with your hurried departure?"

"Well, you're not the only one who has to come up with explanations. My father calls me every Sunday, eleven A.M. on the dot, on my landline. Even when I used to live at my sister-in-law's. It reassures him. A bit like your mother."

"Looks like we're in the same boat," I said with a laugh.

"Yes, but I'm a woman," she said, not laughing.

"Who has to explain herself to her legal guardian," I sneered.

"Exactly."

"See you next Saturday, then?"

"Yes, Saturday. Bye, Mohamed."

What would my cousin think if he heard that I was going out with a girl on whom I had not laid a finger? And that I didn't even know the color of her nipples? A girl who slept in my bed in pink cotton pajamas buttoned up to her chin? who commanded me to keep my underwear on? who got dressed with her back turned to me? who ran home to be there in time for her daddy's phone call?

And what if I offered her a call-forwarding service? I'd pay for it. I'd insist on it.

Fortified by my resolutions, I crawled out of bed and went into the living room. I swallowed a shot of whisky to help me get back to sleep and I went back into the bedroom. After I'd unplugged the landline and switched off the cell phone, I burrowed under the comforter.

When I woke up, it was almost three o'clock in the afternoon. My brother and my brother-in-law must have been at the mosque.

And your mother must be cursing you, whispered the voice in my right ear.

Shit, I swore.

And what if I telephoned my young thing? But I remembered she was with her sister-in-law and she didn't need my help to put up her bookshelves.

What does she want from you? whispered the voice in my left ear.

She's just the girl for him, whispered the voice in my right ear.

And what if I don't see her again? What if, like the forty-something, she disappears before I have time to possess her? And why don't I phone the forty-something, anyway? I could invite her girlfriend along.

And what about Agnès Papinot? whispered the voice in my left ear.

Yes. Why not? I replied. As a pretext, I could say I want to buy an apartment. In the 20th or the 18th arrondissement. Such a momentous decision. She'd arrive by taxi. Scantily clad. The elevator. The mink. Chamonix. Pie in the sky.

I was going hard and my head was already spinning when I saw the pink pajamas rolled into a ball and left on a corner of the bed. I tore off my underwear, grabbed the pajama bottoms with one hand and my cock with the other, and thought of nothing else but breasts that were as round and firm and quivering as a pair of young pigeons.

I slotted the capsule in the coffee machine, he said, put a cup below the spout, and pressed the button. I watched the liquid drip into the cup and thought to myself that I was lucky to have good coffee to drink, and that it was pleasant to see the daylight filtering into the room. Autumn was coming. The days were getting cooler. And the fireplace. All the flames would help. Would kindle. Naked as on the day I was born. Plus carpet. Nest. Little Versailles. Call a chimney sweep. Order firewood. I'm really settled in and, my God, it's in the bag. Or nearly in the bag.

Her name was Djamila. But she went by Jamo. It's more practical, she said. If it had been up to Camus, whose novels she adored, devoured, to baptize the Algerian Arabs, maybe the ones now in France would not be blushing about their names, she said.

Whatever the case may be, she continued, she never showed herself to photographers or critics, who, uncertain as to the exact origins of the "talented Jamo," praised and celebrated her work, comparing it to Frida Kahlo's. And, God be praised, her canvases sold well. Even in New York, she added. Then she filled up our glasses. She liked champagne. Champagne was the only real thing.

Momo and Jamo. That has a nice ring to it, I thought, as I lit a cigarette.

But not for founding a family, whispered the voice in my right ear.

No, of course not, I said.

Can you imagine your kid saying, Hi, I'm Momo and Jamo's son?

No, no, I said.

The woman who will bear your children, with whom you'll celebrate your *Fatiha,* in due time, in the presence of your loved ones and the imam who married your sister to Alain also known as Ali, as well as Driss and his two wives, will not have a nickname. Besides, who, in your opinion, would marry a girl he'd met at a party that was a borderline orgy? And who, without batting an eyelid, took you home? into her bed? Even a Swede in the seventies wouldn't go for a marriage like that. Never mind if the woman in question has talent or travels around the world and all that.

The voice seemed so real, so strident, that I shook my head and waved my arms. And silence returned.

I swallowed my hot coffee down in a gulp and crushed my cigarette in the designer ashtray—a present from my ex-girlfriend Samira, also known as Khadija, that virgin who went to bed wrapped up in pink pajamas and who no longer answered my calls—and I went into the living room.

I put on a record, the same one as the last time she came over, a week ago now, and I listened to the messages flashing on my machine. Five, all from my mother, and I erased them right away.

I took a swallow of scotch and dialed the young woman's number. While it rang in the void, I realized bitterly that she no longer switched on her answering machine, and I hung up. I took a Stilnox and turned off the music. Taking the telephones with me, just in case she happened to be reminded of my existence, I went into the bedroom.

As I pulled off my jeans, I noticed that my underpants were gone. The girl called Jamo had kept them.

"I collect them," she had said, inhaling the depths of my

shorts with a satisfied air. "I love the way men smell here, like toasted hazelnuts . . . "

During foreplay, while she tore off my shirt, then my pants, and finally my boxer shorts, several times over, with that same satisfied expression on her face, she had sniffed me and licked me, taking her time over my cock, comparing it to an eggplant, stroking the perfection of the glans . . . She went on and on, saying that foreskins were great for caresses, any woman would agree, but that coming across a circumcised man from time to time wasn't bad. Then off she went sniffing me again and licking me and lapping me. Warm saliva moistened my testicles, and a slow burn spread through my gonads all the way to my rod, then every square millimeter of my body. But the moment I had (successfully) unfastened her bra, and was starting on her panties, she pushed me away.

It really is a fine one, she said. But it was too big and too long for her condoms. She was about to get her period, she added, and if I penetrated her it would surely start her bleeding, she claimed, introducing my index finger into her vagina, which was indeed tight, but so wet, so warm. A steam room.

Sitting up, she eventually took off her panties and spread her legs. Staring at my rod, while a shadow of extreme martyrdom crossed her large, dark eyes, ringed with fatigue and makeup, she said, "You can look, or touch, or nibble, as much as you want. Take your time."

No sooner said than.

My lips sucked on her clit, my tongue dug about in the depths of her sex. Relentlessly. Indefatigably. You would have thought I was an expert. Never suspecting for an instant that, thanks to her, I was receiving my baptism of flesh, and none the wiser, so to speak, she sighed noisily.

A moment later, assuaged, with the dexterity of a pro she began massaging my sex with her feet and with such fervor that

I felt faint. She then moved my head away from between her legs and, pushing me over onto my back, she grabbed my rod, which was about to explode. What a marvel, she said, sitting on top of me. She placed the glans against her clit, and slid it slowly to the opening of her vagina, ready to put it in, then, changing her mind, she brought it back against her vulva, which was tauter and wetter than ever.

And while I was reciting, in a scarcely audible voice, in Arabic, a passage I had learned years ago, one I thought I had forgotten, my seed splattered all over her tuft, which was not black, but white.

"Next time we'll put it in," she said, wiping herself off with a Kleenex. Then she asked me what it was I had been reciting, it was lovely, could I recite it again?

"What, now?" I asked.

"And the other times," she simpered.

"In Arabic or you want me to translate?" I said, looking at my sated sex, enormous, it's true, but immaculate, unburdened of its knowingly trimmed hairs.

"My Arabic hasn't completely gone to seed, I'm originally from Biskra where, unlike in Algiers, people speak perfect Arabic. Did you know that the Orientalist Jacques Berque learned fluent Arabic while he lived with Bedouins in my region?"

"I didn't know that . . . "

"So, will you recite it for me, the text?"

I cleared my throat and began to declaim: "Every time one sleeps with a *houri*, she is a virgin. The rod of the Chosen One does not decline. The erection is everlasting. To each coitus corresponds a pleasure, a delicious sensation so unusual for this base world that if a man were to feel it on earth, he would fall down in a faint."

"That's hot," she murmured. "Is it in the Koran?"

"It's by a famous theologian and poet who was inspired by the Koran. His name was Abd al-Rahmane al-Souyoûti."

"Is he dead?"

"Oh, yes, he died at least five or six centuries ago."

"Are you a believer?"

"I was. But that's finished. And you?"

"I'm not really sure, but I do sometimes feel like packing it all in—painting, the exhibitions, travel, all the society stuff—to going back to basics. Start with a pilgrimage, to purify my bones, so to speak, and then settle somewhere in a cave or an igloo, to expiate my sins until the end of my days."

"A Sufi life, basically . . . "

"Who's ever seen a female Sufi, let alone a female imam? I'm sure some crazy would tear me to pieces."

"Oh, but you're wrong. I could list over fifty Sufi women from throughout history. From Amina al-Ramliya to Maryam al-Basriya by way of Rabia al-Adawia or Majida al-Qorayshiya. Unrivalled in their devotion, acknowledged and revered by the greatest *ulema* on earth."

"Oh, really?"

"Absolutely. Women who devoted themselves to God, unconditionally."

"Djamila al-Biskriya for posterity," she cried, exultantly. "That's far more honorable than Jamo, at any rate. But my sins are so great that one life would not suffice to expurgate them. Abortions like there's no tomorrow, booze, unclean meat, forgetting Ramadan and all the religious holidays. Not to mention a child out of wedlock . . . "

"He who renounces sin and returns to the Way shall know absolution. For God is mild and merciful," I declaimed.

"But are Sufis obliged to get married?"

"Of course."

"Women, too?"

"A good Muslim woman, like a good Muslim man, is obliged to marry and procreate. And the pleasures of the flesh are not proscribed," I said, giving her a sidelong glance. "Islam is the only religion where sex pleads not guilty," I continued, carefully enunciating each syllable, thus allowing my ulterior motive to filter through, but my semi-mistress did not pick up on it.

"Are you married?" she asked.

"I haven't had time," I said.

"Me neither," she said, thoughtful, "and I don't think it will ever happen."

"You're young . . . "

"Thirty-nine . . . and a half. I'll be hitting forty in just a few days . . . "

"Khadija, the Prophet's first wife, was forty, actually."

"But where can I find a prophet in this day and age?" she said. Without laughing.

I was about to volunteer, and reveal the erudition I had inherited from my revered ancestor, as well as my strong poetic fiber, and tell her that we could become the most famous Sufi couple of modern times, that we could live in a cave or an igloo, and everyone on earth would make the journey to observe us, that we would set the example for the *oumma* of the Rasul, may peace be upon Him, and we would assuage hearts and minds, we would convert millions of souls, and on the Day of Judgment the balance would weigh in our favor, and so on. It was not that I found her beautiful; in actual fact there was nothing exceptional about her, she had neither blue eyes nor the mane of a queen, she was even a bit ravaged, with thin, tiny breasts, more like prunes from the larder than apples from the Garden, her legs were dry with no calves, like the legs of a little girl from the arid regions of the Sahel—a survivor— but she did have something, something indefinable, something about her eyes, something about her sex in my mouth, her hormones making their way into my cerebellum, percussing my pituitary gland. In short, for the reasons I have just enumerated, I was going to submit my application, but, loyal to my (recent) resolutions as an emancipated man, I thought better of it and said, "I've heard there's a prophet in Greenland."

"Who spends his time with a compass in his hand, trying to determine which way Mecca is?" she said with a burst of laughter.

"That's the one," I said, with sudden, inexplicable gravity.

"And converting the Inuit tribes. But because the day is so short in winter, the five prayers have to be recited without taking a breath in between. And in summer, because the sun hardly sets, they are so far apart that people get tired and get fed up waiting. So the proselyte got discouraged and went back to Paris, where he had to deal with his mother's whims, she's a widow who used to be very pious and a real stickler for principles, the daughter of a Sufi master, in fact, who moved in with her son to remove some spell or other that he was under, and then discovered the lights and the splendor of Paris, and began to hang out with the concierge of the building and changed course overnight, turning into a die-hard Westerner—"

"I didn't know he'd come back," I interrupted, somewhat dazed.

"So you didn't read the book right through to the end?" she asked.

"Which book?"

"*The Sultan of Saint-Germain.*"

"Uh . . . no."

"You don't know Loubna Minbar?"

"I've heard the name . . . "

"She got along really well with Driss until the novel came out, because your cousin has been stubbornly insisting that he is the main character. Which is why they've fallen out, I think. But your cousin is no Islamist. He's an inveterate hedonist."

"A true Muslim, a good Islamist, is a hedonist . . . "

"Whatever the case may be, to get back to your cousin's paranoia, if it were me, frankly, I wouldn't give a fuck about finding myself in a book. And anyway, I expect to, every time

I open a book by Loubna Minbar. Diddly-squat. Although I've known her since childhood."

"Oh, really?"

"We were at school together in Biskra. I knew her family, too. In those days her name was Louisa Machindel. At school, and then later at boarding school in Algiers, we made fun of her name, we changed it to Machandelle or Fernandel, and we even made up rhymes and shouted them in the stadium at the lycée, something like this: *Machindel made a scandal with the vandal.* Which humiliated her beyond belief. To the point where Bencouscous or Boumerguez would have been dream names for her, so she told me. The Arabic teachers only spoke to her in French and wouldn't let her say anything, and they even let her skip class. I can still hear one of them saying, You may leave now, Miss Machin-thing, the headmaster won't be informed . . . You have to admit no matter how you try to pronounce her name in Arabic or in Berber, it makes no sense. Even today, there are those who won't miss an opportunity to try to make her squirm, like that guy who shouted in front of a whole bunch of people that she wasn't even Algerian, and he called her Madame Alas."

"I've already heard that somewhere . . . "

"You're bound to have. He wrote it in a book. And because Louisa's family didn't have a *zawiya*[1] the way most families in North Africa do, they say that her ancestor was a Christian from the West, that he set off for the East and converted when he married a Muslim woman, from Ethiopia or Somalia, then he came to Algeria with his Negress to scatter his offspring. Which could explain the fleshy lips and flat nose and dark dark skin that Loubna inherited. At any rate, I knew her really well, we were close friends, she lent me books, she came to my

[1] In North Africa, a Sufi religious community's mosque, especially when containing the shrine of a holy person (T.N.).

place, I went to hers. One of my brothers was crazy in love with her. It's true that when she was young she was a knockout. Tall, slim, a dream body, a set of teeth to die for, skin like a baby. You wouldn't know to look at her today, would you?" she asked, as if I already knew you.

Later on, she continued, her brother found you at the medical school in Algiers. But he was already engaged. His mother, who generally couldn't stand for her eldest daughter to have girlfriends, actually liked you, she said. She welcomed you with open arms. And it was in a way thanks to your parents that she came to France. She was fourteen, she had just had a rotten summer. It was a long story. Through her brother, she found you in Algiers where, twenty years or so ago, she had ended up teaching at the fine arts school. At that point you had quit your medical studies and started studying literature, and you were working for a newspaper. And living in a house by the sea. Alone. Against your parents' wishes, and your neighbors', and everybody's. And it caused you no end of trouble. But together you made good use of the garden—barbecues, suntanning on the terrace, until it all fell apart and it was run for your life, fear, blood, the arbitrary nature of things, so she described it. Without emphasis or pathos. And then she lost track of you once again, until she found you completely by chance in Paris.

"As soon as she recognized me—it was at a party at Driss's—she said, 'Hey, I was just thinking about you.' She was working on a novel . . . "

"*Djamila and Her Mother?*"

"Have you read it?"

"Uh, no."

"After that, we met every day, brunch at a sidewalk café, dinner at her apartment, she was working on her novel like a crazy woman, her right hand was oozing, even cortisone didn't help . . . And then, just before *Djamila and Her Mother* came out, boom, she vanished, not a word. Moreover, no one sees her anymore. Not even Driss, who never found out what had driven her to steal his life. They say she moves around all the time and when she's in Paris she goes into hiding."

"To write?"

"And she's just had a kid, a girl, she named her Pauline but no one has seen her. Madness, don't you think? She swaps Machindel for Minbar, and then burdens her kid with a name like that. Just imagine the poor kid in Algiers or Tunis or Cairo with her little Arab face saying, My name is Pauline . . . Not one of *us* has ever given a Christian name to a kid. My daughter, for example, who was born in Sydney, with a Catholic father as white as snow, is called Yasmine. Hadda's daughter is called Nedjma. Fatima, who is pregnant at last, has already chosen the names. At birthday parties, you can easily number four little Yasmines, just as many Nedjmas and Myriams, Marwans and Samis, Elias and Yanis. But Pauline—what was she thinking? If you want my opinion, Loubna knows she's sold her soul to the devil, and that's why she isn't showing her face. And anyway, when it's all over, she moves on . . . "

"When it's all over?" I said, struggling against dizziness, blaming it on the champagne that we were drinking like soda pop.

But she did not answer my question.

"Anyway, I am very flattered to have been compared to a *houriate-al-jana*," she said, in Arabic.

Then, gulping down her drink, she jumped out of the bed and disappeared behind the bathroom door.

When she came back, I'd already forgotten our chatter, her blah blah, and I was beginning to fall asleep, sure of spending the rest of the night in my hostess's warm sheets, sure we'd have another round of little fantasy, one where she wouldn't stop me at the entrance to her pussy.

But she shook me gently and asked me to leave. She needed a few hours' sleep before taking her plane later that evening. And then, once she'd confiscated my boxer shorts, with their evocative smell of toasted hazelnuts and all that, she went with me to the door, and talked to me again about her birthday, said she really wanted me to be there, she would be having a party in two weeks' time, when she got back from Mexico, where an artists' foundation, she said proudly, had offered her a stay in a house not far from where Frida, the very same, used to live . . .

Too bad, I thought, lowering the blinds in my bedroom. Then I switched off the nightlight and fell into bed, my curiosity aroused: one day I would count the number of items in her collection. Did she also keep strings?

You're on the right path, whispered the voice into my left ear.

Well, I don't know about that, whispered the voice into my right ear.

I'm not having any more of this, I murmured, drifting off to sleep.

I was dreaming of a field of eggplants, he said, when the ringing of the phone woke me up.

"Good morning, my mother . . . "

"Well well, you're not whispering anymore."

"The cat ran away . . . "

"What a pity."

"Yes, it's a pity . . . "

"And you're not up yet."

"I went to bed late . . . "

"Late, late, that's all you ever say."

"It's Sunday, my mother . . . "

"I will not hang up until I've had a chance to speak my mind."

"Yes, my mother . . . "

"Now that you're living in Paris like a parish priest, no one ever sees you. What will our neighbors think? Do you know I am counting the days? Do you realize you left in July?"

"July of which year, my mother?"

"What do you mean, which year? You're making fun of me now, Mohamed son of el-Mokhtar!" she barked, in Arabic.

"Forgive me, my mother. I was still in my dream."

"Well, you'd better wake up from that dream of yours. Your sister, unlike some, comes to eat my couscous every Sunday, and her husband says his prayers."

"I know, my mother."

"If I'm telling you again, it's for your own good, so that you'll start again. Your brother-in-law isn't even a Muslim, and he—"

"He is, now."

"But his parents aren't. They're not even Christian. They're nothing at all, atheists up to their eyebrows. God protect us, and he didn't know the first thing about Islam. Not only does he continue to go to the mosque, but he attends the *Halaqa* with pleasure, he doesn't miss a single lesson, he chants the *moutaawidhates* in Arabic, and all in one go, and his face radiates the light of Paradise, and soon he'll recite the *Sura al-Baqara* like a master. Your grandfather would have been proud of him, believe me."

"I believe you, my mother."

"If that son of *roumis* has joined our fine religion, it is thanks to that master. Without the religion he gave first to me, then to you, and which I continued to hand on to you as best I could, your sister would have just gone her own sweet way in this debauched country. She would have been like all those girls who go off with infidels and have no fear of the wrath of Allah."

"Yes, my mother."

"She would have been just like her sister who's rotting in Blida, or the other one, that wretch who called her son Pierre. Did you know, by the way, that his name is Pierre?"

"No, my mother."

"I found out through the neighbor's daughter, the one who was with her at the lycée, actually, but she made a good marriage, she did, and is raising her children to keep to the straight and narrow."

"Yes, my mother."

"Can you imagine the shame that this will bring upon us? If she hadn't been born here, we would have taken her by force to Blida. But she'll pay for it. On earth and before Allah."

"Yes, my mother."

"I've heard that you see her."

"See who, my mother?"

"The non-believer."

"No, my mother."

"That's what else my neighbor's daughter told me. She saw you together, she said, in Paris."

"She was mistaken, my mother."

"And to think you are the only one of my children who had a real religious education. So did it all go for nothing? Am I going to roast in hell because of you?"

"Don't worry, my mother, I am neither a non-believer nor an apostate. And I never will be."

After a sigh of relief, my mother said, "We're waiting for you, apple of my eye. Your brother and your brother-in-law are going to the mosque. I've washed and ironed your clothes. You'll join them, won't you?"

"Yes, my mother . . . "

"And I have a surprise for you, apple of my eye."

"What sort of surprise, my mother?" I sighed.

"Nothing you could ever imagine. In any case, it's not a fiancée. You'll see, my son . . . "

I crawled out of bed and went into the living room. I swallowed a shot of whisky, to help me get back to sleep that much more easily, and I went back into the bedroom. After I'd unplugged the landline and switched off the cell phone, I burrowed under the comforter.

When I woke up, it was past two o'clock in the afternoon. My brother and my brother-in-law must have been at the mosque.

And your mother must be cursing you, hissed the voice into my right ear.

Shit, I swore.

After my shower I drank a coffee and settled at my desk. I opened the computer and went through the notes I'd made, higgledy-piggledy, for my book.

I also noticed that every Monday I had chronicled every one

of my single-man Sundays, along with all the evenings I'd spent over the course of these last three months with the fresh young thing who no longer returned my calls and who had not switched her answering machine back on.

I opened a file, determined to write to her. It was time for an explanation. We'd gotten off to a really good start, the two of us. Yes or no? Did she not have my spare set of keys? Who did she think she was, anyway? The slave Roxalane?[1] I was not some sort of dog. I was a sultan, in actual fact. Then I remembered that she had never given me her exact address. And the rue Notre-Dame-des-Champs was endless. I called information to no avail. Her number was unlisted. I deleted the letter and sat for a long time looking at the plane tree growing in the courtyard.

Persist, hissed the voice in my right ear.

He does have other things to do, whispered the voice in my left ear.

Patrol the sidewalk up and down the rue Notre-Dame-des-Champs. Keep a watch out for her in all the nearby shops. Outside her school, in the libraries of Paris. Be a man, a real one, hissed the voice in my right ear.

And what if I really was going crazy?

I switched off the computer with the firm intention of speaking to my psychiatrist about these voices. Besides, I hardly had any Stilnox left.

I went round in circles and called the boxer-shorts collector. She didn't feel like going out, and she was getting ready for her trip, she moaned. Then she reminded me of her birthday party. I mustn't forget, she'd be delighted, little *houri*. Etcetera.

"You know the way, now," she said. "You can call me when you get here so I can tell you the code. See you soon, Mohamed."

---

[1] The second wife of Suleiman the Magnificent, the first Russian slave in history to be married to a sultan (Mohamed).

Satisfied with my initial sexual performance, proud of this upcoming date, I wrote down in my diary that I must urgently buy a pair of boxer shorts, the finest ones in Paris, and they would be my present . . . And to hell with the daddy's girl who never answered my calls, and who kept my keys. She had never entrusted me with her own keys, or even let me visit her apartment, and she'd gone so far as to refuse my help when she was moving in.

I opened my cell phone. I typed, *Please return keys. Mohamed,* and hit "send." A moment later, *Message received* flashed on the screen.

The following Sunday, he said, when I closed the door to my apartment, the reminder note where I'd written LUNCH AT MOTHER'S caught my gaze.

Then I thought about Nadia or Samia. I can't remember which. How could I remember a name that I could hardly hear when we'd been introduced? I myself must not have said it a single time.

What I do remember is that she was as blonde as a field of wheat. Rather ripe, the wheat. But what does it matter. Had she not kept my cock down her throat? For an entire hour. With an eye on the clock. It happened in my car, and I'd have to clean the backseat without delay, before it started smelling of sour milk, I thought, picking up the cigarette lighter from the table by the entrance.

One hour, I thought, lighting up a cigarette and heading for the kitchen. My ex, that virgin who blushed down to her pussy if I walked through the apartment naked, that girl who never returned my calls, who unplugged her answering machine and kept my keys—which is why I hadn't invited the woman with the bleached hair to my place—the two or three times she'd actually tried hadn't lasted more than three seconds. And our affair hadn't lasted three months.

How can you qualify her as an ex? whispered the voice in my left ear.

Before spelling it out:

An "ex" is someone with whom you have copulated your fill.

An "ex" is someone who has emptied you out according to the rules.

An "ex" is someone who used to hang around in the apartment if not naked at least in the extravagant negligee that was a token of your generosity.

An "ex" is someone who gave herself to you indefatigably, without keeping tabs.

An "ex" is someone very different from that chick who disappeared without a warning.

That's true, all very true, I grumbled, staggering to the kitchen.

I placed a cup under the spout of the machine and pressed the button. The green light started to flash. As soon as it stopped flashing, I put in the capsule and pressed the button, which again began to flash.

I watched the liquid dripping into the cup and I told myself that I was lucky to have good coffee to drink, that I would gladly offer one to the blonde from earlier on, the one who had made use of her mouth, her tongue, and her throat, I recalled with delight while staring at the foam thickening in the cup. But the same woman explained to me that her husband would for sure detect any smell of sex on her, and she had refused to let me penetrate her.

That creature whom you will not introduce to your mother, hissed the voice in my right ear.

Not on your life, I replied, swallowing the hot coffee. Forty years old. A perv. A married perv.

At which point I played back the calls flashing on the machine. Five, and all from my mother, which I immediately erased. I swallowed a Stilnox, picked up my cell phone, in case the virgin Khadija-Samira-Roxalane happened to call, and headed for the bedroom.

Before getting undressed, I hunted through the pockets of my jeans to find the contact info for the blonde with the black roots—I'd met her at a gallery opening that Driss had dragged me to, assuring me that I would not go home alone, and let that little student go fly a kite, he sniggered. That pious little hypocrite, looking for a husband, he scoffed.

"I know her sort only too well, girls who come here from their village, supposedly to study," he said. "They play the emancipated type and all that, but the minute they find a guy like us, they get their hooks in, and presto!"

"I don't think she's like that," I protested. "All she cares about is her studies . . . "

"You think she would have spent entire weekends at your place if all she cared about was her studies? Or that she would have offered you an ashtray from Conran if you were a supermarket stock boy? Or if you were living at your mother's? Or if you had kept your suburban accent? She would not even have looked at you, buddy! Where did you meet her, anyway? Huh? Saint-Germain? At the Flore, right? That's where they go hunting for guys like us. Can you picture her hanging out in some place like the Café des Amis in Ménilmontant? You say she never said a word about marriage. That's just tactics, cousin, they are as sly as foxes, those little cuties. She might even make you believe she's a virgin up to her eyebrows. And the day before the wedding, she'll spread her legs for the best hymen restorer in Paris. I've been around them, you know, those petty bourgeois chicks from Algiers, and I nearly fell into the trap. Your little white goose wants only one thing, for you to go up to her nabob of a daddy with a ring and some splendid prospects for his darling daughter. I don't know if she told you, but her father is the biggest importer of beer and baby milk in the country. Before that, he was a bigwig in government, known as the white wolf in Algiers, even here. *Le Canard Enchaîné* published an article about him."

"You're mistaken all around," I said. "Her father was a

simple fisherman. And the man she looks to as her father is a playwright. Her sister-in-law told me."

"Whether he's her father or not doesn't change a thing regarding her intentions—her sole interest is your bohemian immigrant life. I had a good look at her at the Flore, you know; with her little well-brought-up airs and graces, she wouldn't even look at me, as though I was the resident scumbag. I'll bet she tried, all casual like, to remind you of the values from the home country, I'll bet she was cooking up couscous and *chorba* for you, and breezing into your place with *makrouts* and baklava from La Bague de Kenza, I'll bet she even ironed your clothes and tidied up your kitchen so that you could sit there all cozy watching *Stade 2*. They'll do that even if they don't live with you. And she would never live with you without a marriage certificate. Besides, those girls set themselves a deadline. If, at the end of three months, there is no sign that they're headed for marriage, they vanish. As if you'd never laid eyes on them."

Other than the fact that she wasn't the daughter of a big wig, Driss was speaking the truth. She would stand there indignantly examining the packets of pure pork ham decorating my fridge, and ask about my ethno-culinary tastes, then cook me up lamb *tajines* and *chorbas* and grilled-pepper salads. But she also ironed my shirts, and advised me to wear this or that tie, and she brushed my suits. And it was with a gleam in her eye that she loved to hear me talk about my work at the bank, about the contracts I was signing with major multinational corporations, about my knowledge of the stock market . . .

Whether she was aiming for marriage or not, she was barely twenty-five years old, she was a virgin, she was cute, she came from a good family, she was a future astrophysicist, she spoke Arabic and observed Ramadan—so I have to admit she did suit me, or at any rate she would have suited my mother, who would have given her a ceremonial welcome . . .

But the whole business didn't even last three months, retorted the other voice. And you don't even know the color of her nipples. And your cousin is right. As we speak, you sit here moping, while the firefly is surely off bantering with a boy her age. Maybe even a real born-and-bred Frenchman, with a foreskin thrown in.

Enough, I cried, and from the back pocket of my pants I pulled the contact info for the woman with the oh-so-welcoming throat. I left the paper out in plain sight on my night table and I could feel my cock swelling.

I picked up the pink pajamas, which I now kept hidden under the right-hand pillowcase—the concierge probably couldn't figure out what was going on; when she came every Friday to clean my apartment she would put the pajamas back in place, though she'd never even caught a glimpse of their owner, or any other woman for that matter, and she had stuck Mohamed Ben Mokhtar on my letter box, and, logical conclusion, must have thought "Mohamed Ben Mokhtar" was my secret lover—and I thought of nothing but the round and firm and quivering breasts . . .

No sooner was I in my dream, he said, than the ringing of the phone woke me up.

"Yes, my mother . . . "

Cut the conversation short. Hang up. Disconnect. Go back to sleep.

"I hope we'll see you today, you haven't forgotten, you won't forget to come and eat at home . . . "

No, I wouldn't forget, I had even written it down in capital letters on a sticky note by the door. I had written it down because my sister, the pious one of course, had informed me that last Sunday my mother had cried all through the meal. She was losing weight before my sister's very eyes. The fact that I never turned up didn't help matters—she was pitiful to look at, and she interrupted the meal to say, "Only your brother is missing, the apple of my eye, who lives like a priest in Paris. And he must be wallowing in filth and buried in dust . . . " And so on, went my sister, holding back her own tears.

"No, I haven't forgotten, my mother. I'll be at the house before noon . . . "

"But it is noon!" shouted my mother. "We're here together to break the fast. Have you forgotten Ramadan? Have you forgotten that today, October 9, is the fifth day?"

"Already?" I said, biting my lip.

"What do you mean, already?"

"The ninth of October . . . "

"Your brother-in-law, Ali, may God protect him, has

already begun to organize our trip to Mecca, my son. The Paris mosque has a very good package on offer. An entire month, room and board and transportation. A week in Medina, and three in Mecca. It won't be cheap . . . "

"You can tell me about it when I get to Saint-Ouen."

"Get here just a bit before it's time to break fast, so we can talk calmly. Thanks to your car, your brother is already back from the market."

Clean the backseat of my new car. Before it starts to stink. Before going to Saint-Ouen. When they take a look at it, my mother, my brother, my sister and her pervert husband might recognize the smell of semen.

"I have to wash my car," I said automatically.

"You can do it here, my son, your brother will help you . . . "

"I have to hang up, my mother, so I can get ready . . . "

"You do that, my son. We're expecting you. I'm waiting impatiently, apple of my eye. And, in addition, your brother's fiancée and her parents will be there. After we break fast, we'll all go to the mosque on rue Jean-Pierre-Timbaud, for the *tarawih* prayer. You'll join us, won't you?"

"Yes, my mother . . . "

"And if you have someone, my son, don't hesitate to invite her . . . "

"I have no one, my mother. Not yet . . . "

"That girl you told your sister about. Isn't she Algerian?"

"Yes, my mother. But she's thirty-four."

"Your sister said she was a student in astrophysics, preparing a dissertation on the planet Venus or something like that."

"That's right, but she's old, my mother."

"The mayor's daughter is still waiting for you, my son . . . Your brother's fiancée's parents will eventually get tired of waiting . . . "

"So let him get married, my mother . . . "

"Not on your life! What would people think? That my eldest son has something wrong with him!"

"People have more important things to worry about, and I'm worn out, my mother . . . "

"You are bewitched, my son. Last week, I wanted you to meet a good Moroccan woman who came all the way from Carcassonne just to remove the spell. That was my surprise, my son. Alas, if the disenchantment is to work, we have to wait until the end of Ramadan. She promised she'd come back and take care of you as if you were her own son. You'll do what she says, won't you, my son?"

"Yes, my mother . . . "

"I'm sure it's that thirty-four-year-old woman who's bewitched you, my poor boy. I always told you, as they get older they turn into perverts . . . "

"Yes, my mother."

"And you haven't even purified your apartment. That apartment where you live must be full of filth and dust . . . "

"Yes, my mother."

"You should have sacrificed a chicken at least, and coated the corners of the rooms with henna, and we should have gotten together around a couscous and left the candles burning until morning. None of that was done. I should have taken care of it. But I don't even know where you live. And you moved out, leaving me with the fait accompli. Is that true or not?"

"It's true, my mother."

"And how are you breaking the fast? With soups from the supermarket? I even wonder if you're fasting, my son . . . "

"What an idea, my mother . . . "

"It was just an idea, my son. I'll go now but try to get here before the others . . . "

I hung up, repressing a burp with an acid taste. Why had I forgotten about Ramadan? My sister had called me on my cell phone, she was so distressed by my mother's crying and her health, so she should have reminded me, she's the pious one, the blessed among her sisters, the one whose opinion I had asked for regarding the fugitive. In any event, if I had been forewarned, I would have stopped drinking alcohol and I would have performed my ablutions in time. At least one week before the start of the fast.

What is the point of purifying your body and your mind? whispered the voice into my left ear. Because, henceforth and forever, you will no longer need to fast. Not even out of solidarity. Or respect for anyone at all.

A free man, I thought jubilantly as I left the bed and went into the living room. I swallowed a shot of whisky, to help me get back to sleep that much easier, and I went back into the bedroom. After I'd unplugged the land line and switched off the cell phone, I burrowed under the comforter.

When I woke up, it was nearly eight o'clock in the evening. My mother, my brother, his fiancée and the family of his fiancée, my sister and her husband, the entire tribe, must have been in the midst of their Ramadanesque prayers, there in the 11th arrondissement.

And your mother must be weeping and cursing you, hissed the voice in my right ear.

Too bad, I said.

I took a shower and drank a coffee. I got dressed and called the girl from the night before, Samia, Safia, Nadia, whom I cordially invited to dinner. She couldn't, her husband had just returned from his business trip, she explained apologetically.

I switched on my computer and printed out my notes. Enough to throw together a chapter, I thought, as I reread them. After which I filed them under "Novel," along with the little bits of paper that contained dates, names collected here and there, plenty of material with which to structure and build my tale, I thought gladly as I stared at the rustling foliage. Then I switched off the machine and walked around in circles, not knowing how to rid myself of the anxiety that was slowly and ineluctably constricting my thorax.

Go find them at the mosque, hissed the voice into my right ear.

Enough! Enough! I wailed.

I swallowed a big glassful of whisky and got back into bed, determined to see my psychiatrist no later than the very next day and talk to him about all this hissing and whispering which, to this day, when I am not careful, still irritates my ears.

The sun had risen, he said, when I closed the door of my apartment. I collapsed in the armchair and my gaze immediately landed on the sticky notes where I had written BREAK FAST AT MOTHER'S. SET ALARM. UNPLUG TELEPHONE.

Then I thought about the girl I had just left. Tall, a bit androgynous, as russet as an autumn leaf, she had admired my cock, she had weighed it and touched it, stroked it and caressed it. On the sofa bed in the guest room at the painter's—the one who collects boxer shorts, and who was celebrating her birthday in splendor, and who'd hardly said hello, Ciao, Mo-a-med, so glad you could come, and she had scarcely glanced at my bottle of champagne and bouquet of roses, which she had thrust into the arms of a guest who was passing by.

In short, she greeted me as if nothing had ever happened two weeks earlier, in these very premises where she had aspired to Sufism and where, this evening, she only had eyes for this handsome Mexican who was hot on her heels all evening, and who looked like neither prophet nor poet, I noted bitterly.

If walls could speak, I thought fretfully; then Driss, turning for a few moments from a tall, flamboyant mulatto, said he wanted to introduce me to "an old acquaintance," as he called her.

Fatima Kosra, but her friends call her Fatie, a peerless lawyer . . .

My cousin Mohamed Ben Mokhtar, but his friends call him Momo, one of the most sought-after financiers in all the realm . . .

Very happy.

Delighted.

Thus, my expensive Ralph Lauren boxer shorts ended up in other hands, those of a real redhead, born in the Kasbah in Algiers; she owed her freckles and her pale skin to her Ottoman ancestors, she told me as she caressed me, refusing however to go any further, explaining that she did not want to disturb the baby. You understand? Because she was pregnant, she said while I ejaculated into her hand. Two months. If it was a boy, she would call him Yacine, like Kateb, and if it was a girl, Nedjma, like the famous novel by Kateb, and she would not waste her time afflicting her child with a white name, unlike Loubna Minbar, who may have had her reasons, among others to thumb her nose at that guy who, before a whole crowd of people, had shouted that she was not even Algerian, and had called her Madame Alas, then branded her an alcoholic, a bitch, in other words, a renegade, a traitoress . . .

"It's an obsession," I said.

"Would you like it if someone called you Monsieur Alas? Or Lush? Or Loon?"

"No," I shuddered.

"The Barbarians are cutting our throats, raping us, disemboweling us. Civilized people—my apologies to those who don't deserve it—are humiliating us, denigrating us, driving us up the wall. Like the men in my country. And beyond my country. Do you remember that guy, a so-called civilized man, who'd been raised on the principles of the Republic, and who said, referring to Ségolène Royal, This is about politics, not a beauty contest. Proof that stupidity is universal," she added. Poor Olympe de Gouges and her *Declaration of the Rights of Woman.*

Then, when we heard that the last of the painter's guests were leaving, she told me one of the stories making the rounds of the patios in the Kasbah.

It was the story of a woman whose husband was absent for

two whole years. This was in the days when people rode to Mecca on camels. When he came back, the husband saw that his wife was with child. What is the meaning of this, woman? asked the husband. The wife replied that the child was truly his, may Allah be her witness, conceived two years earlier, but that it had fallen asleep to await the father's return. The man went off to see the imam. The imam confirmed what the wife had said, and all's well that ends well.

This story had always fascinated her, she told me. As a lawyer in Algiers she used to refer to it to plead the case of women who were accused of adultery. Since the birth of Islam, I then said to her, to the present day, we have invented stories like this to avoid the worst. Was she familiar with the book entitled *The Ruses of Women,* by a certain Abd al-Rahîm al-Hawrâni? No, she replied, somewhat surprised. Well, I continued, give or take a few details, you can read the same story in that book, and many others that have saved lives and marriages.

"So have you read *The Sultan of Saint-Germain?*" she asked.

"No," I replied. "But I keep hearing about it wherever I go."

"The main character is forever quoting the author you just mentioned. What's his name again? Abd al-Rahîm? As well as a certain al-Souyôuti. And other Arab theologians and poets . . . "

"And your husband?" I said anxiously, fearing that a colossus might suddenly appear out of nowhere to smash my face in over *almost* nothing.

"I'm not married," she said.

"Bastard," I said, without thinking.

"What do you care!" she said with a laugh.

"All the same," I said.

"I'm the one who refused to get married."

"Oh, really?" I said, looking at my sleeping cock, which was enormous, it's true, but absolutely immaculate, unburdened of its hair.

"You know, at my age, you don't go getting yourself weighed down with a husband. And you know, when I was in Algiers, my worst fear was that I'd get pregnant. It wasn't easy to get the pill, you had to know a doctor or a pharmacist. Or borrow a marriage certificate discreet as could be to get the pill from the mother-and-child-care dispensary, and they'd only hand out one box per woman per month. In short, it was a major hassle to fuck in peace," she added. "So you see, a pregnancy in the heart of the Kasbah—my mother would have buried me alive!"

And then one day, so it happened, she was pregnant. She had just passed her bar exam. Her mother, who thus far had been so proud of her daughter's untarnished career, trusted her and gave her permission to go away on vacation when she asked, to a friend's place in Oran. In actual fact, the friend in question was waiting at the other end of town.

"She'd organized the whole thing—the doctor, a real fake marriage certificate, and she'd managed to extort money from the guy who'd gotten me pregnant and who, naturally, had done a bunk. But the day of the operation we found out that the doctor was in prison for practicing illegal abortions. I thought I'd never get out of this nightmare in one piece," she sighed. "Time was passing and my tummy was getting rounder before my very eyes, when we finally managed to get the address of a back-street abortionist. I'll spare you the horror of it—hemorrhaging, the consequences . . . "

Four years later, in the midst of all the upheaval, at a time when you had to run for your life, she left Algiers. On the plane she ran into a childhood friend.

He lived in some sort of hotel in the 18th arrondissement, where he was the manager. At his request—what better could she ask for?—she moved in with him, and their relation ended up in marriage, to the delight of her mother and brothers. And to her own. Religious ceremony, humongous couscous, civil ceremony beneath the tricolor flag, it was your regular Liberty-Equality-Fraternity. Honeymoon by the sea in Vendée. A fairy tale, she added.

"But Rachid always found some pretext to get out of the appointments at the prefecture, where he was obliged to be present for me to get my paperwork in order. The actual fact of the matter was that he was waiting to make sure I was really pregnant. All my eggs were blighted, and I'd expel them as soon they were conceived. Five years later, despite all my efforts, no children."

Then, when she was going through yet another miscarriage, her husband began to change. The modern man she'd met on the plane, who liked his muscadet and his seafood, who took her to the Basque country where she could lie on the beach topless, who made love to her beneath a tree in the forest of Fontainebleau, was now letting his beard grow, was welcoming pilgrims at the hotel, had transformed the bar into a mosque, replaced the furniture with carpets, painted the walls green, the same green you see in all the mosques, and he had hung *suras* and other images from the Kaâba and Medina here and there on the wall.

"I was in really bad shape and he wanted to put me on a plane and send me back to Algeria. Eventually I ran away. We got divorced and I never saw him again. Anyway, it's a long story."

And then, she continued, she moved in with a girlfriend, the very woman who had called her daughter Pauline, whom she had met seven years earlier in the Barbès *hammam*.

"It was Sunday. I had just had my umpteenth miscarriage and I decided to purify myself and drown the nostalgia for my work and my friends and the family I'd left behind that was eating away at me. In the vapors of the steam room I met Loubna Minbar. She wasn't very talkative, though I have to admit I didn't let her get a word in edgewise; she listened to me and nodded and from time to time she stared at my right foot, the crippled one. You see, I'm missing a toe," she told me, removing her shoe. "In short, I had a lot on my plate—my husband, my life in Paris, living as a semi-clandestine, and all the reasons I left Algiers."

Fear, the arbitrary nature of things, blood, she had said. Unemphatically, without pathos.

"After that, we stayed in touch. I often went to visit her in her apartment on the rue des Martyrs, near Abbesses. Sometimes she'd organize a dinner where her old girlfriends from Algiers would come by, and male friends too, and that's how I met Jamo, Hadda, and even Samira, the little amnesiac."

And when she separated from Rachid, her novelist friend offered to help her out. At her place she met a Norwegian, a widower in his sixties who was childless and had no intention of having any children. He was the correspondent for a weekly paper in Oslo, and he lived in a dream apartment, sixteen hundred square feet, rue Pigalle. His neighbors were a famous actor and his wife, who were in the middle of a divorce, and their conjugal strife spilled over onto the landing, as they squabbled over a worn sofa, or a clock that wasn't worth a penny. Such was the atmosphere in which the Norwegian asked her to marry him. They hadn't even known each other a month.

"I can't say I was dying of love for him," she said. "He was on the ugly side, he smelled like an old goat, but my papers still hadn't come through, I was fed up with coming and going to the prefecture, fed up with Bureau 8 where they treated us like lice. So I accepted his proposal."

They were married at the Norwegian embassy and, very quickly, she was granted the nationality. And in no time at all she had a French residence permit valid for ten years. It wasn't issued by Bureau 8 but by another office for high-end immigrants—smiles and bowing and scraping were the order of the day. Whatever. A last she could move around however she liked, pound the Parisian pavements, get her fill of the cafés and stores, go out at night, and take the metro without fear of being taken away and sent home on a free ticket without so much as a farewell or a suitcase or a present, like some piece of scum.

Of course her mother and brothers knew nothing about her new marriage, something they would have condemned out of hand.

"As time went by," she said, "I began to appreciate my husband, almost love him. I have to admit he treated me like a gazelle. We went to restaurants, to the theatre, we entertained politicians and journalists and humanitarians—they came to taste the '*cuscus* prepared by his *vife* who *vas* russet as an autumn leaf, but a real Algerian,' bragged the Norwegian."

In actual fact, she smiled, as her mother had never taught her so much as how to boil an egg, the couscous in question had been delivered by "Allô-Couscous."

Everything was hunky-dory, and her kind-hearted new husband, without grumbling, agreed to support her for the time it would take to validate her degrees. But no sooner had he seemed perfectly contented with the dormancy of her libido—temporary, she assured him, a dormancy she attributed to a nervous breakdown but, to be honest, she said again, she found him repugnant—than he suddenly got it in his head that he wanted children.

"Just one, he begged. When I told him that it could wait, he countered that he was getting old, that I wasn't all that young myself, and that he could not bear the idea of dying without having fulfilled his desire to be a father. He was the son and grandson of an only child, and after him there would be no more Søren Fosnes Hansens. Finished. No more. Dustbin of history. So I told him the truth. That all my ova were blighted, that it was one of the reasons for my divorce . . . Two weeks later he took off with a young thing who gave birth to his son before our divorce was even finalized."

The alimony was ridiculous, hardly enough to keep her in cigarettes; the apartment the Norwegian had left behind was exorbitant, so she moved back into the two-room apartment with Louba Minbar, who in those days was writing *The Time of Punishment*.

"As she was an insomniac, she gave me her bedroom. For over three months all I did was eat and sleep, and I only went out to buy cigarettes or potato chips. I watched television ad nauseum, and waited for God knows what. A miracle. Or death. Then my savings ran out, and I shook off my lethargy and began to look for a job. I did all the little odd jobs you can think of—nanny, cleaning lady, check-out clerk, market vendor."

Until the lawyer, she continued, who'd dealt with her two divorces, wrote to her one fine day. He needed an assistant. He worked with Saudi companies and he was interested in her background. She couldn't believe her eyes; she read the letter ten times. Then she took over the novelist's apartment—her friend had moved away without leaving a forwarding address. Because, she added, when it's all over, she moves on.

"When it's all over?"

Sidestepping my question, she said, "Once I'd been hired and the trial period was over, the lawyer screwed me, of course, just once, the guy was okay, and he's still pleased with my work and I'm pleased with the job."

In the meantime, bolstered by her financial independence, crying now and again whenever she saw a commercial for Evian, avoiding parks with sandboxes, struggling against the nostalgia for something—maternity—she would never know, she took on more lovers, with the goal, however unlikely, of finding Mr. Right. Because, two thousand kilometers from there, her mother had not stopped harassing her by phone, incriminating her, telling her to get married and put an end to her life as a "divorcee," that all her cousins were mothers and some of them were already mothers-in-law, almost grandmothers.

"'You need to remarry,' she would weep. 'Never mind if he's not Algerian, so long as he's a Muslim. And if he isn't a Muslim, it's no big deal, you'll convert him. And if he doesn't want to convert, never mind, my girl, but just be sure to name the children properly, you'll bring them up on the right path, you'll celebrate your sons' circumcisions in the proper way, you'll watch over your daughters' honor. Allah will look after His own.' Then, last year, at the end of the summer, my mother died. I went to her funeral with a terrible feeling not of grief, but something else. It was more than a feeling, it was a sensation of lightness that I had never known, that I had never thought I could attain, as if I were sprouting wings, as if by burying my mother I was being unburdened of some sort of secular cope, and at last I could escape, a woman without chains, without master, the woman I have become . . . "

Just after she came back from Algiers, a lawyer recently hired by her boss, younger than herself, fell in love with her. And it was mutual. Ten months later, no more period. It was menopause, she thought. But her doctor ordered a pregnancy test. Po-si-tive. It took hours for the truth to sink in, days before she actually realized what was happening.

"And there we are," she exulted, caressing her stomach. "And I am doing everything I can to make sure my baby doesn't let go. That's why I don't want to be penetrated. You understand? Even though—and this you can believe, with the rush of hormones and all the rest, any pregnant woman will tell you as much—it's not that I don't feel like it."

"And the father?"

"Dismissed," she said, with a glow of pride. "Well, he's the one who broke it off; he was shocked that I refused to live with him. No matter how I explained that I loved the idea of being single and pregnant, that I was living out a sort of fantasy, that we could wait until after the birth to get married, nothing doing. He called me a crazy old woman and broke it off. Having said that," she continued, "all the dreams I have now are about pregnancy and they're all mixed up with my past. I'm on the rue Didouche-Mourad, the longest one in Algiers, the one that goes from the Grand-Poste to the Ecole des Beaux-Arts. Do you know Algiers at all? Anyway, there are a lot of people in the street, and I am wandering around with nowhere special to go and suddenly I see how incredibly huge my belly is. For a moment I think I haven't digested the last five meals I've eaten, and then I have to face the truth: I'm pregnant, and it's visible. I'm pregnant and my mother will bury me alive. Then without leaving the dream I realize I'm in Paris, and I have an official status known as 'lone parent,' and no one at work is the least bit bothered, except the genitor himself, who has just resigned. And maybe you . . . "

"Come off it!" I said, while the voice in my right ear was telling me to get the hell out of there.

It was still hissing along as I lowered the blinds in my bedroom, unplugged and disconnected the telephones, and fell flat on the bed, all out of sorts and dressed like a cowboy.

Get away from those women who refuse to give themselves up on the pretext that they're lesbians or virgins. Or that they're expecting their period, or a kid. Even the least talkative of them, the one who didn't have *a long story* to tell, even she rejected you.

They're lost women; they fled the South but now they've totally lost their way.

As a result: sheets never rumpled. Never soaked.

That's how far you've come, oh Sultan of Saint-Germain.

I wanted to be further than this by now.

It was final.

I had to find the young thing. Whatever the cost. Patrol her
street from one end to the other. Keep a lookout for her in the
shops. In front of her school. In the local libraries. Put the ring
on her finger. If need be.

What's the point? I shouted. She's gone.

Call Agnès Papinot. On the pretext of an investment. Invite
her to dinner. Put the ring on her finger. If need be.

And so on and so forth, until a drug-free sleep took over.

PART THREE
A MADMAN'S BANQUET

"No books are committed
without a motive."

LOUBNA MINBAR

When I woke up, it was well past two o'clock in the afternoon. I had slept a long, deep, uninterrupted sleep. A first for me. No Koranic school. No morning prayers. No shopping at the market. No phone ringing into my dream, Aren't you up yet, my son?

I stretched, and cracked my neck and my knuckles, breathing in and out as if I had just discovered oxygen, then I left the bed, and my clothes, which I shoved into the laundry basket.

I let the bathwater run, swallowed a glass of orange juice, made myself a good strong coffee and took it into the bathroom. I lit all the candles that were set along the edge of the bath and slipped into the warm, sudsy water.

An hour later, smelling of luxury eau de Cologne, meticulously shaven, with a bath towel round my waist, I strode barefoot across my hardwood floors, made a second coffee as robust as the first, and settled into the armchair facing the balcony, with my eyes on the Paris skyline.

As I stared at the bluish plumes that rose above the roofs, I thought I should make a fire. The chimney sweep had come on Friday, the wood had been delivered and piled in the loggia, or so the concierge had told me, for it was she who had dealt with the chimney sweep and the delivery man. But there was no wood in the loggia. Or anywhere else. Never mind, I thought, going back into the living room. I'd call the concierge. Maybe she'd gotten the wrong Friday. Or maybe I'd mixed the days up.

I drank my coffee and smoked one cigarette after another. My thoughts were stalled. As I didn't know what to do to entertain my mind, I began to inspect the apartment—the closets, the dressing room, the library, the hardwood floor, the sparkling windowpanes, my ironed shirts, my suits neatly on their hangers . . .

My mother, who imagined that the apple of her eye was up to his eyebrows in filth and evil spells, would have been impressed, I thought, as I removed my towel and put on a track suit.

Ready to get to work, I opened the file marked "Novel," but my notes were nowhere to be seen.

Second disappearance, I thought mechanically. First the wood. Now my notes. Or maybe I had never printed the notes out to begin with? But I remember printing them perfectly well. Just as I recalled the quality of their contents.

I switched on the computer. There they were. In the right file. With a sigh of relief I clicked "print" and poured a whisky, which I sipped as I smoked a cigarette. When the machine had stopped its creaking, I picked up the sheets of paper. They were blank. I checked the ink level and started over. Not a line. Not a word.

Quelling a rush of anger I went back into the living room. I poured a second whisky and began to mentally construct the opening pages of my book. He lived in fear of collapse. It inhibited him. The fear of collapse inhibited him. Friday, June 23 of the year 2006. Right after the *khutab*. Compass in hand, Driss sought the direction of Mecca in vain. The horizon. White. Bluish. Glacial. Then come the lost women. Each with a long story to tell. He couldn't remember a thing about those stories. Or hardly a thing. Or maybe everything.

After I'd filled my glass to the brim, I went back into the study. By hand I wrote, "Tangled up in lies. Prisoner of his past, guarding his secrets jealously. He liked his booze. Couldn't sit up straight in front of the machine. Alone, with cirrhosis of the liver. Two opposing destinies meet. Implosion for one. Explosion for the other. The rust of time. Sex is life's curse. Lucky Driss. Left without warning. Drifting endlessly. In a bottomless pit. What a terrible feeling, all this weariness, and you're not even sure you exist. Driss the bigamist. Blessed by his loved ones. Left without warning. But why?

"An external experience, not internal. In other words, an experience stemming from others and not his own personal quest, which is why his faith failed to attain its potential and turned around and went back to the place they'd gone to get it for him in the first place. The abyss of the void.

"Venus the enigma. Inhospitable Venus that orbits backward. The lost women. The voluble women. He nodded his head as he listened to them spouting their insane talk. Moving through a world where ecstasy and anxiety are formed, the two men went away in silence. One into the darkness. The other into ice and fire."

It was at that point that I remembered the pink pajamas underneath my right-hand pillow, where the concierge had carefully tucked them away. But they were gone. I looked in the closets, the dresser drawers, the wardrobe. I rummaged through the laundry basket. In vain. Could it be that she had come by to collect them in my absence? She would have left the keys with the concierge. Hadn't I sent her a message to that effect?

I called the concierge. "Has a young woman, a girl, left a set of keys with you? She's a brunette, with big eyes and long wavy hair. A fairly ordinary face . . . "

Silence.

"Neither tall nor short, slim nor round, often wearing jeans and a white shirt."

Silence.

"Make an effort, Madame Lisa. It's *very* important."

"I assure you, I can't imagine who . . . And there was never any question of me calling the chimney sweep," she replied. "Not this year, in any case." But she would take care of it, first thing tomorrow.

She didn't know anything about pink pajamas. How could she, she said briskly, when at my request she had returned the spare set of keys, and besides, she reminded me, she was no longer doing my housecleaning.

"Really?" I said.

Confused, I hung up.

I dialed Samira's number. *The number you have reached is no longer in service. Please make sure you have the right number in mind.*

Already! I exploded. So I called my cousin. I needed his advice. Or in any case to speak to him. But no one replied.

So I dialed Agnès Papinot's number. Of course, Monsieur Tocquard. She had several things she could show me. That she was sure I'd like. Let's meet, shall we say, tomorrow? At the Jean-Pierre-Timbaud agency. In the 11th arrondissement.

She dictated the address.

Rolling her syllables.

Real and authentic, I said, staring at the bluish plumes caressing the roofs of Paris.

I was not yet in my dream, he said, when a ringing that I didn't recognize, which must have been coming from the neighbors' door, or so I thought, woke me up. I tossed this way and that to try to find the right position for going back to sleep. Just as I was shoving my head under the pillows, the ringing began again. It was at my door. Who could it be, on a Monday morning? The concierge with a package? The mailman with a registered letter? But the concierge was efficient and discreet: when there was a parcel, she always left it just outside the door. And she had the power to sign for registered letters.

And what if she was at my door? That young woman? The one who disappeared—with my keys? And now she had come to get her pajamas. But she wouldn't ring. She would open the door, the way she had always opened the door, entering the apartment like a gazelle . . .

And what if she had lost the keys? And what was I to do with Mademoiselle Papinot, who was sleeping the sleep of the blessed on my sofa? She had missed the last metro, and before so doing she had wrung my confessions out of me, and then my secrets. And now she knew everything about me. From my birth to the day I walked into the real-estate agency. And all my recent tribulations. My encounters. The women who appeared and disappeared. The one I cared about most, the gazelle, the Turkish delight . . .

She had listened to me with unflagging interest, though

whether she was nodding out of compassion or weariness, I know not. Just as I had listened to those talkative women in order to hasten the end of their stories. Hoping, thereby, to attain my ends.

And then, just as I was starting on my umpteenth whisky, could scarcely hold back my tears, and was on the verge of collapsing, she ran her fingers through my freshly straightened hair, and confessed that she had been aware of my lubricious intentions the day we were going through the inventory of fixtures, and had been flattered. Oh really? I said, sure that we would end up spending the night glued to one another.

A moment later, I was signing and initialing all sorts of documents. I had become the happy owner of a house on the rue Jean-Pierre-Timbaud. Right near the mosque. Two stories. A little garden for the children. It's perfect for you, Monsieur Ben Mokhtar, Mademoiselle Papinot had said, looking at the candle that was dripping great drops, illuminating not the scene which I alone had anticipated and in which my guest had shown no interest, but the one where all the week's negotiations were finally being concluded, and the contracts were being signed, endowing me with a dream house, susurrated the real-estate agent, who had brilliantly attained her own ends. A house I had not visited, only seen on photos. Be prepared to do some work on it. Of course. Not lived in for years. But a veritable jewel, said Mademoiselle Papinot, all aflutter.

In short, I was in a right fix, here in my purple satin sheets. An arm and a leg. Dry. Smooth. Chaste.

All that for this.

The ringing began again and I sprang out of bed. I threw on a T-shirt and some boxer shorts, walking on tiptoe so that I would not wake up Mademoiselle Papinot, and as I walked past the living room I closed the door, then turned to the front door.

Through the spy-hole I saw the concierge, and with her my

sister, the blessed one, and my heart skipped a beat. They have come to inform me of something inconceivable, I thought, struggling not to pass out. My mother in the hospital. Alone. Dead of sorrow. Already in the morgue.

He lived in fear of collapse, I kept repeating to myself, bracing my back against the wall.

I finally opened the door. My sister was not wearing a scarf or a *jellaba* but, thank God, there was nothing in her expression to indicate the occurrence of a misfortune. And the concierge was smiling maliciously.

"Here he is," she said.

Then she turned on her heels.

"May I come in?" said my sister, stepping into the hall.

"What are you doing here?" I asked, following close on her heels, catching her just as she was placing her hand on the door knob to the living room.

"Some welcome!" she flung at me, over her shoulder.

"I have a guest," I whispered.

"As I thought, and that's why I'm here. To warn you that Mom is coming."

"Mom who?" I cried, forgetting the woman asleep in my living room.

"Your mother, my mother, our mother," said my sister as I shoved her toward the kitchen.

"But she never comes to Paris!" I said, lighting a cigarette.

"You've never invited her, poor woman," said my sister with irony.

"Nor have you," I retorted.

"I go to her house, at least."

"She could have let me know . . . "

"You never listen to your messages. Even Alain called you."

"Alain?"

"Ali, if you prefer," said my sister, sweeping the kitchen with her gaze.

Then, without any warning, she informed me that my mother had decided to move in with me for the time it would take to rid me of my spell and get me married, and that she would be coming with a Moroccan woman, some sort of witch, a very efficient witch, whom my mother was counting on to have everything done before the Great Hajj, in other words before the Eid al-Adha on December 20.

"December 30," I corrected.

"December 30, that was last year. The lunar calendar loses ten days. You're better situated to know that than I am . . . "

"I am?" I said, somewhat dazed.

My sister contemplated the table cluttered with the remains of last night's dinner—oyster shells, wine glasses, empty bottles—and said, "You're still drunk, brother. But you should have enough time to get your wits about you, she's not coming until the day before the Eid . . . "

"When's that, the day before the Eid?"

"In a week."

As I was letting out a sigh of relief, my sister added, "In the meanwhile, I'll help you clean up this dump. You can tell it's the apartment of a boy whose mommy never instructed him in the use of a dust cloth. And when I think that the mommy in question is convinced you're living with a thirty-five year old woman . . . "

"Thirty-four," I corrected, remembering the lie I'd concocted for my mother during one of her long-drawn-out Sunday calls.

"Whatever the case may be," said my sister, "she wonders whether you haven't already had a child with this woman, and whether you didn't break it off with us for reasons that have something to do with our cousin Driss."

"I have neither wife nor child. And no intention of having either. Where would I find the time? As for my dissidence, so to speak, it has nothing to do with Driss," I said.

"Well that's lucky," said my sister. "Poor Driss . . . " she added, sorrowfully.

"Driss is very happy," I protested.

"Let's hope so . . . "

"No father or mother, and accountable to no one," I said, thoughtful and envious. "Our mother panics over nothing. For the pleasure of panicking, I suppose . . . "

"Well, the fact remains that you don't do a thing to reassure her, you never pick up the phone, even on Sundays, you switch off your cell, we're not allowed to call you at work, and the rare times you do call her, you just serve up the same old stew, 'Sorry about last time, my mother, I was on a business trip, my mother, I was working all night, my mother.' You think it's fun for a mother who has sacrificed—"

"I never have time—"

"She prays from dusk to morning, she's decided to fast for the *dahr*. You have to have an iron faith to fast all year round. In short, she can't stop crying and saying over and over that it's all her fault, and she has to expiate it. She's aged, she's lost weight, she's always out of breath," sighed my sister.

My head in my hands, to try to staunch the flood of tears welling in my throat, a dull anger blurring my vision, I said, "And Alain-Ali? What about him? Is it just a pose?"

"A pose for survival. I didn't want to make the same mistakes my sisters made. That would have just finished our mother off. But Alain really is sincere. He wouldn't have gone along with the circumcision just to please me. And he really does practice his faith, in depth—he learns about everything. And besides, we're virtually separated, he has another woman . . . "

"I suspected as much, I thought he was a strange guy . . . "

"Frankly, I don't care one way or the other. On the contrary, he has liberated me the way no one else ever could have. And besides," she said with a laugh, "I've met someone myself."

"I don't want to know." I cut her off.

"I can see you're as rigid as ever."

"Who gave you my address?" I asked curtly.

"Zoubida. I had to beg her. Get her worried that maybe you had done something irreparable. I've never stopped seeing her. Unlike you: you've shown her no sign of life for over a year."

"I can't keep up with the time . . . "

"And your conquests distract you from your family obligations. Incidentally, who is your guest?"

"She works in real estate. We've been working all night."

"*Tabtab,* as our old lady would say."

"Well, she is sleeping on the sofa . . . "

"You're going to have to wake her up, she has to leave so I can clean," she said, shoving the last plates into the dishwasher.

"Go ahead," I said, slumping into a chair.

"Okay," said my sister, reluctantly.

A few minutes later she came back into the kitchen and informed me that my guest was no longer there. That she must have slipped away discreetly . . .

"Already!" I said, leaping up from the chair.

"Good job, too," said my sister. "I have no intention of spending the night cleaning up your house."

I slumped into the chair again and stared at the horizon, struggling in vain against the flood of tears that was overwhelming me.

"Can you fix us a coffee?" asked my sister.

"Because you're not fasting?" I sobbed.

"No, and you?" she laughed, starting the dishwasher.

"For me it's not the same," I said, wiping away my tears.

"Why isn't it the same?"

"That's my business," I answered, starting the coffee machine.

My sister said nothing more and drank her coffee down in one gulp. Then, as she looked around her at the kitchen, she began to lose her temper.

"Get out the vacuum cleaner, the dust rags, and all the cleaning products you can find in this dump."

"My apartment is spotless," I said indignantly.

"I'm sorry, but this place is disgusting. It's just as Mom imagined. Can't you see the cockroaches parading behind your fridge, and all the dirty saucepans, and the empty cans, and the dust bunnies that have hopped right into the kitchen? There are books and papers scattered all over the hallway and the living room, and packs of cigarettes and empty bottles wherever you step. And I haven't even seen the bedroom . . . I wonder how on earth she agreed to come have dinner here."

"Who?"

"The guest who vanished."

"I'm getting married at the end of Ramadan," I said.

"To the girl who slept in the living room?"

"To the mayor's daughter."

"The one from Fouka by the Sea?"

"The one from Fouka by the Sea."

"All this for that," said my sister, raising her eyebrow.

"I don't want her moving in here."

"Who?"

"The mother."

"Don't worry, she won't stay forever. Just long enough to get rid of the spell," she said, leaving the kitchen.

She took a look around the living room and exclaimed she had never seen such a shambles, and she wondered how on earth I could live in such mess and filth, and how my guest could last even one night in the stench and dust, and where on earth she could even have lain down, and then she opened the door to the balcony.

She picked up the empties that were scattered here and there, and the books and pencils and paper, and she moved the furniture around and put it back in place, and she shook and plumped the cushions, and ordered me to bring her the vacuum cleaner right away and the rags and the cleaning products and the garbage bags . . .

Hours later, when everything was finished, and the apartment did shine like new, my sister said, "Do you know Loubna Minbar well?"

"By name . . . "

"Only?" she said, astonished.

"Yes. Why?"

"How do you explain the presence of all her books here? Several copies of each?"

"What books?"

"Loubna Minbar's books. Those are the only books you have."

And she listed the titles. *The Sultan of Saint-Germain. The Kidnapper from the House Across the Street. The Time of Punishment. Djamila and Her Mother.*

"Anyone would think you spend your time reading these books over and over. There are notes on every page, passages underlined. Something about a swallow, and a woman with a crippled foot, and a young amnesiac . . .

"There's a manuscript with that title," she said, glancing over at a ream of paper carefully piled on the coffee table. "The dedication is astonishing," she added, with sudden, deep sadness.

Trembling, I picked up the manuscript and read, *My thanks to Driss for his trust and his outspokenness.*

I felt suddenly, overwhelmingly jubilant.

"It *is* Driss, then," I whispered, turning the pages.

"Unfortunately," murmured my sister, wiping away a tear.

"Apparently he recognized himself in the story," I said.

"He read it?"

"Everyone's read *The Sultan of Saint-Germain* and everyone knows that Driss is angry with Loubna Minbar for stealing his life," I said.

My sister shot me a glance, half-anxious, half-intrigued.

"Because Loubna Minbar wrote that, too?" she said, staring at the manuscript I still held in my hands.

"Who else would have written this book where she talks about our cousin as if he were an Islamist who's almost lost his mind, exiled in Inuit territory, looking for Mecca and struggling with the time zones at the North Pole?"

"It's an image," said my sister.

"Insanity."

"I knew Driss was well-acquainted with that woman, that they spent a lot of time together, but I didn't know anything about this text," said my sister, thoughtful.

"And I wonder how it ended up here, at my place . . . "

"If the text really is by Loubna Minbar, as you seem to think, you must have found it at Driss's when you were getting rid of his things," she sobbed.

"What things are you talking about? And why are you crying?" I asked, irritated.

"It's just that I can't seem to forget June 23, 2006."

"At some point or another, the apron strings must be cut," I said, thinking of the day when, determined to break with my own mother, I had gone into the real-estate agency . . .

"But the way he did it . . . "

"Never mind the way. It happens even to women. Even to you," I said, taking in her bare head and legs.

"Right after the sermon . . . So young and handsome. So full of life. Two widows. Four children."

"Who are you talking about?" I asked, just as her cell phone began to ring.

"It's Kenneth," she said, blowing her nose. Then, suddenly radiant: "I have to go. Don't forget to take the garbage bags down. There are a ton of them. It will take you a while."

"Who's Kenneth?" I asked, raising my voice.

"My English lit teacher, a specialist on Christopher Marlowe. A great guy. Remember to call the old lady, you can tell her that I came by to see you, that will reassure her a bit, but above all don't breathe a word about my life, or about Driss, I'm counting on you," she barked, before slamming the door.

I wanted to catch up with her, but the elevator was already on the ground floor. I grumbled and suppressed the anger I could feel welling up in me, and went to sit facing the roofs of the city as I tried to piece together my days from the time I left my mother's until my sister's unexpected arrival.

Nothing but the life of a troglodyte.

All that remains is to get back in touch with your origins. Return to your upbringing, your values.

That's right. Dead right.

Don't spoil it all, Arab. All has not been lost.

Shit, I swore.

And went to lie down.

At dawn, before they'd even drunk a coffee, he said, my mother and her acolyte were building a fire in the fireplace, in order to use the embers to fill a brazier. Once they'd had their coffee, the fumigations began—benjamin, musk, amber, root of I know not what tree with invincible properties, according to the Moroccan woman—filling the apartment until the odors spilled out onto the landing.

I had ended up taking my vacation earlier than planned, and I spent it locked in my room, reading, thinking, scribbling, writing, ordaining that I was not to be disturbed for any reason. Except, obviously, for those manipulations where my physical presence was required.

At dusk, at the end of the day, my mother came to scratch at the door.

"It's bath time," she proclaimed.

A bath scented with orange flower water, to which was added drops of holy water from Zamzam, imported from Mecca, and essences of all sorts. With my private parts hidden beneath a loincloth, I plunged into the bath, beneath the grave gaze and incantations of the disenchanter, incantations that my mother echoed with equal gravity.

Once I had dried off and gotten dressed, I carried my dinner back into my lair. At twilight, the two women lit forty candles, then coated the baseboards, along with the soles of my feet, with henna.

At the end of the fortieth day, the Moroccan woman

decreed that the spell was broken. We sacrificed a sheep, not in the bathtub, but at a specially conceived abattoir. Half of the beast was given as an offering to the mosque on the rue Jean-Pierre-Timbaud, and the other half was cut up and placed in the freezer compartment.

Taking with her a quarter sheep and a few wads of euros extricated from yours truly's bank account, the Moroccan woman departed. My mother stayed behind. When she saw the stupefaction on my face she came out with the excuse that she had *things* to take care of in Paris.

"And Mahmoud?"

"Mahmoud is a big boy. Besides, he's getting married soon."

"Before me?"

"So?"

"What will people say, my mother?"

"People have other fish to fry, my son . . . "

And the nightmare continued.

Equipped with a cell phone, which she handled like an expert, she called me to inform me that she wouldn't be back for lunch, that she was at the *hammam*, or in a store, in the check-out line . . . Or that she was at a girlfriend's, Madame Lisa's. She was looking after her daughter. Probably until late that evening.

I was as sure of the order of events as of the succession of day after night, night after day, the rotation of the earth around the sun . . .

All is not lost, Arab. Control and vigilance, said the voice, trying to rouse me.

But I could not halt my downward spiral.

As my mother still did not want to go home, I prolonged my vacation, devoting my time to *The Sultan of Saint-Germain*, reading and re-reading, underlining phrases, jotting them down, analyzing them, taking note of anything that clearly indicated that this "Sultan" had absolutely nothing to do with me. That it was indeed about Driss, and Driss alone. For need I remind anyone of the fact that I had neither the desire nor the inclination to end up in Inuit territory. Nor anywhere else, other than in my nest. My little Versailles. A free man, that is what I was. A free man, privileged and civilized, and I intended to remain so.

And a pox upon Greenland.

A pox upon glaciers.

A pox upon the inferno of Venus.

That's right. Dead right, I muttered, sinking ever deeper.

When I suddenly noticed that my mother was no longer unrolling her prayer mat, I went into a panic and informed her that I was ready to marry, my mother . . .

"Do you have someone in mind, apple of my eye?"

"The mayor's daughter, my mother."

"The one from Fouka by the Sea?"

"Do you know of another?"

"My son, my adorable child."

"I've taken a special leave, which will give me the time to organize both the wedding and our departure for Mecca. Mahmoud and his wife. Ourida and Ali. My wife and I. And you, of course . . . Is this not what you wanted, my mother?"

"I am exhausted, my son. But we'll talk of it again."

Yawning, leaving me with my herbal tea and the television, she went into the bedroom from which, once the witch had left, she had summarily evicted me.

Am I not your mother?

The next morning, I performed the morning prayer out loud, so she would hear me and so that, reassured about the fate of the "apple of her eye," she would face the facts and go home, back to her young son, to her own walls and devotions. But at around nine o'clock, my mother was not up yet. I went over to the bedroom. I placed my ear against the door, hoping to hear her breathing, or moving around. The door was so thick that no sound could penetrate, neither her breathing, nor any noise that might indicate she was alive, so I pushed it open.

My mother was sound asleep, wearing a red silk nightie and a beatific smile on her face.

"Aoudhou-billah-mina-achaïtan-errajim!" I conjured Satan at the top of my lungs, and with all my strength.

Startled, tugging at the comforter, my mother in turn began to scream.

"What happened?"

"You are almost naked, my mother."

"Forgive me, my son."

"It is past nine A.M., my mother."

"I was awake all night long, my son."

"Doing what, my mother?"

"Reading, my son."

On the nightstand was a book that did not belong to me.

"I'm taking out a new lease on life, my son. And it's exhausting . . . "

She buried her head under the pillows and went back to sleep until noon.

I am lying down in my "temporary" bed, staring at the plumes of smoke above the roofs, when I hear my mother's voice.

"What do you think?"

I turn my head: she is standing on the threshold, her eyes large and dark, her eyelids creased, her hair long and wavy, neither gray nor white nor even black, but as blonde as a field of ripe wheat . . .

"Well?"

I am speechless.

"You don't like the dress, is that it? Or the makeup? Or the hair color? Louisa helped me."

"Who's Louisa?"

"Your concierge."

"Lisa. Madame Lisa."

"Madame Lisa is just to keep her position. Like you, Basile I-don't-know-what . . . She's one of us. She's been living in France since—you know when. Fear, the arbitrary nature of things, blood. And her apartment—you have to see it to believe it, it's overflowing with books, my son. Piles all the way to the ceiling. She's the one who lends me the books I devour night after night. In exchange, I babysit Pauline for her."

"I know who she is. Her name is Minbar. Loubna Minbar. She's a writer."

"Her name is Louisa and she is not a writer. She's a concierge."

"What else are writers, they're concierges, my mother, they feed on other people's lives."

"I can assure you she is not a writer, poor woman. She inherited all those books from the previous tenant, who moved to a retirement home . . . And in the evening, just the way I, your mother, used to do, she's bent over her sewing machine, she spends her nights embroidering tablecloths, caftans, caps, sheets, and she's ruining her eyes and her hand, it's so bad she sometimes bleeds."

"A typewriter, my mother. She's bent over a typewriter, not to embroider but to mess with people's lives. That woman is a public menace. It's not only her hand she's ruined, but everything she touches. Driss spent time with her, too, and she stole his life, my mother. Without even condescending to provide him with an explanation. She vanished. When it is all over, she moves on."

"I don't want to hear about that non-believer, what he did."

"It happened because of that Louisa who calls herself Lisa and who is none other than Loubna Minbar. A woman who rejected her family, and only meets them to find fuel for her literary projects. She'll do the same with you, my mother. I have all her books. I don't know how many times I've read them."

"I know, my son. Your sister Ourida talked to me about them. She's thrown them out."

"I know her characters by heart, down to the most minute detail. I've even met them. Women who've lost their way, not one who could save one another, and it's all her fault. Anyone who comes near that woman, that stealer of lives, is bound to lose their mind. That's the fate that awaits you if you go on seeing her, my mother."

"You're imagining things, my son, that poor woman is struggling to make ends meet to raise her child. No father or mother. Just her and her daughter in this world full of sharks where she's forced to sell her embroidery for nothing to the big couture houses . . ."

"She stole my notes and in their place she left some sort of text dedicated to Driss."

"You'd do better to get some air . . . By the way, I'll be back late tonight, I'm having dinner with a friend. A West Indian woman I met at Zoubida's place."

"You are seeing that non-believer again?"

"A mother is duty-bound to forgive . . . And why so much spite? She's your sister, your blood . . . She's going to organize a lovely party for her son's circumcision, and she's going to take the opportunity to change his name. She has chosen Mohamed. In your honor."

"May Allah reward her with good."

"You should get out more, see your friends. I don't want my presence here to upset your habits."

"I'm organizing our trip to Mecca, my mother. And my wedding."

"You spend your time admiring the rooftops of Paris, my son."

"That's just your impression, my mother."

"As for the pilgrimage . . . we're still young. We have our whole life ahead of us to cleanse our sins."

"Yes, my mother."

What good would it do to lecture her? She was losing her mind, but it wasn't her fault. No, it was with that opportunistic, subversive, manipulating, intriguing transplant and stealer of lives with whom I had to settle my accounts.

Oblige her to re-write the book. To restore dignity to all those she has misrepresented, starting with Driss, whom she portrayed as a sybarite and a villain.

Lock her up. Gag her, if need be.

But what would the neighbors think?

That a Muslim was living among them?

But violence was not programmed in the genes of my wise ancestors. Like my grandfather, I am incapable of attacking even the vilest cockroach invading my apartment.

I need to come up with a stratagem, and implement it in a subtle way.

Stop my mother's metamorphosis.

Cancel my exile into Inuit territory.

Thwart that woman's premonitions.

Get things rolling with the mayor's daughter. Organize the wedding. Speed up work on the house with garden. Get the Renault Espace. Rings and wedding bands. Solid gold bracelets. Gold-embroidered caftans and robes. Wedding ceremony. Ululation fit to bleed out a woman's tonsils.

And my life as a free man?

"Fine, my son," said my mother, as if I had just approved of her reasons for canceling the pilgrimage. "And anyway, the pilgrims are about to turn around and head for home."

"And the mayor's daughter, my mother? Our promise? The house I just bought?"

"I didn't want to tell you, but she got married. Since you couldn't make up your mind, her parents gave her to another family."

"I already sent in my notice to move out of this apartment. The work on the house on rue Jean-Pierre-Timbaud is finished."

"You'll be comfortable there, my son. You'll eventually find the right girl. That little blonde from the agency, that Agnès you often talk about, you should introduce her to me. She would be perfect for you . . . "

"She's a Christian, my mother."

"She belongs to the People of the Book, my son . . . As for your apartment, I'd be happy to take it over."

"How will you pay for it?"

"God will provide."

"The rent is really high, my mother."

"Forgive me, my son, but I came across one of your pay slips by chance . . . "

"So?"

"Well, someone who doesn't have a family, my son, can very well start helping his mother who has sacrificed everything for the sake of the apple of her eye, and who has never asked for a thing in return. Look at you, my son, you're a sultan. Thanks to whom? Thanks to your poor mother, who also deserves to live. I still have some good years ahead of me, my boy . . . All my life I have satisfied your every whim. With you I've toed the line, to the detriment of poor Mahmoud, who spends his time cooped up with his mother or at the neighborhood mosque. And his fiancée has just broken off their engagement. Without warning. No explanation. If only someone could reason with him and persuade him to Gallicize his name, he'd blend in better."

"He cares about his principles, my mother."

"Faith inhabits the heart, my son."

"He must be suffering in your absence, my mother."

"If you could just get him to come along with us, my sultan . . . "

"Your dress—"

"You don't like it, is that it?"

"Too short. Too red."

"Who does it bother, my son? We're in Paris, my boy, in Saint-Germain."

"You'll remember to take it off before the guests arrive," I said off the top of my head.

"Are you expecting people?"

"Forty pilgrims."

"I'll put the veil back on to greet your guests, my son."

"That's right, my mother. What would they think of us, otherwise?"

"Yes, my son."

I had just emerged from my dream, he said, when the phone rang. I lit the lamp and read the name on the screen.

"You've reconnected your phone, my son."

"Good morning . . . my mother."

"You sound out of breath, my son."

"I just had the most terrible nightmare."

"Recite your *moutaawidhates*, my son."

"I have, my mother."

"Your sister told me you were a bit tired, my son. But I'll be there the day before the Eid. The Moroccan woman will come with me, and will stay with us as long as it takes . . . "

"It's pointless, my mother," I said.

"There's a spell on you . . . You're over forty years old and you're still single . . . And your brother's fiancée's family is starting to get impatient."

"I've made my decision, my mother. I'll get married when you want, however you want."

"Do you have someone in mind, my son?"

"The mayor's daughter . . . "

"From Fouka by the Sea?"

"Yes, my mother."

"But she got married!"

"Already?"

"You wouldn't make up your mind, so her parents gave her to another family. I told you, in one of my messages."

"Just like in my dream."

After a long silence, my mother said, "I'll be there in two days . . . "

And hung up.

I got out of bed. I took a shower. I drank a coffee and switched on the computer. After I had printed a list of all the painters and decorators in Paris and the entire region, I began to make my calls.

It's not complicated, I said to the guy who agreed to start work the very next day. Nothing but green. The same green that you find used in . . . Bring your entire range. I'll choose the right color.

Then I called the Salvation Army, and gave them the details of my bequest: a leather sofa and armchairs, tables, a desk, a bookshelf, lamps. All luxury items, trendy, with the invoice to prove it. Not for sale. A bequest, I repeated. The woman seemed satisfied but, she said, they didn't have a truck available. Could it wait a few days? It's today or never, I decreed. She hung up on me.

I called the town hall to inform them that I would be placing furniture, a lot of furniture, on the sidewalk that night. Then, finally, the concierge.

"I'd like three strong guys to take my furniture and leave it on the sidewalk. I'm changing the décor in my apartment. I've got guests coming. Pilgrims. And I'm getting married, to a woman carefully chosen by my mother. An Algerian who's less than twenty-two years old. We'll be living in the house on rue Jean-Pierre-Timbaud. Two stories and a little garden. Mademoiselle Papinot, from the Sèvres Agency, knows all about it. But I'll keep my apartment. Any trips to Greenland or Venus are out of the question. The sultan of Saint-Germain will end his days in this building, on rue Saint-Placide. Just like Huysmans. Got that? And don't you dare go anywhere near my mother. Understand?"

Silence.

"Understand, Madame Loubna Minbar?"

"I understand, Monsieur . . . "

And then, as if I had just been relieved of a great burden, I felt as light as froth and, whistling, I looked up the number for "Allô-Couscous."

For forty people. Day after tomorrow. Okay?

No problem.

Add ten portions, while you're at it. For the beggars, I whispered.

All right, said the woman. Fifty portions of royal couscous, that it?

That's it . . .

And for dessert?

It's dinner for people of the faith. Ascetics. No dessert.

Then, catching my breath, I phoned my young brother. A dinner with forty pilgrims, Mahmoud. For the Eid, I said, sincerely happy to hear his voice, and I suddenly realized how much I'd missed him.

Recalling that he had never been to my place, I dictated the address.

"Ourida already gave it to us," said my brother, apathetically.

"He who renounces sin and returns to the Path shall know absolution. For God is mild and merciful," I declaimed, thus lending credibility to my redemption. "Inshallah, my brother?"

"Inshallah," he said.

For a moment I thought of inviting my brother-in-law, the convert, and my sister, the blessed one. But then I remembered her falseness, and for fear that she might ruin my plans I scrapped the idea.

After that, I took a shower and brushed my teeth; my beard was growing before my very eyes, as was my hair: my curly locks needed a good cut at the barber's, and my eyes were shining with that particular gleam of anticipation of victory over she who claimed to transform people and their destinies, the world, and the direction of Mecca.

Driss, with his compass in his hand, I sniggered.

He who laughs last laughs best.

I got dressed and left the house. I ran into the concierge, did not greet her, and went out into the street. A moment later I was in the carpet store on the boulevard Raspail, the one I had stood outside when I was moving into my place, when I had felt a bit lost in the alleyways of my neighborhood.

I chose a dozen *kilims*, an equal number of Persian rugs, and thirty or more cushions that would go well with the carpets. The shopkeeper could not believe his eyes.

"Can you deliver everything tomorrow?"

"To be sure," he said.

His hand, when he took my check, was trembling like a leaf.

At the taxi rank outside the Hôtel Lutétia, American businessmen were talking loudly. I shoved past them and jumped into the taxi as it pulled up.

"Barbès," I said.

Once I was there I asked the driver to wait for me. I did my shopping in no time at all. Representations of the Kaâba and the mosque in Medina. *Suras* written in golden lettering. Copies of the Koran. Prayer beads. Prayer mats. And of course an immaculate white outfit, almost as well made as those of my own mother's fabrication. And I found myself thinking about her. I bought some scarves and *jellabas*. Endless quantities of them. In case the premonitions turned out to be . . .

"Is this for an association?" asked the shopkeeper, helping me carry the bags to the taxi.

"It is to save my mother," I replied.

"Well done, my brother."

"I'm not your brother," I said. "I am a free man," I added, waving to him through the window as the taxi pulled away.

Two days later, he said, by the end of the afternoon, my walls were green, the green you see in the mosque, and the engravings were hung, the carpets were unrolled, the cushions were scattered. Once I had performed my ablutions and trimmed my beard, I put on my new outfit and opened the front door so that my guests could come in the way, in the old days, one entered the home of my august ancestor.

Sitting cross-legged with my back to the wall, facing the entrance to the living room, with the Book open on my lap, I began to chant the *Baqara*, the longest of the *suras*, the one my brother loved to recite with me.

Good, very good, hissed the voice in my right ear, just as my mother suddenly appeared on the threshold to the living room. Followed by a woman. Then my brother. And finally his fiancée. Unable to believe her eyes, my mother burst into tears. A flood of tears. And my brother, too. But silently. My future sister-in-law, troubled, looked down.

I held them in my arms in turn, and ignored the woman who was with them; I wished them a joyful holiday of the Eid, my mother, a joyful holiday of the Eid, my brother, a joyful holiday of the Eid, my sister.

"The pilgrims will be here soon. Forty, for the peace of our ancestors," I said, inviting them to sit down.

Breathless, her eyes wild, my mother murmured something in my brother's ear. Then she began to weep again.

"I'm going to ask for help. All alone we won't manage," said my brother.

"There's no need, Mahmoud," I said. "We're going to be served by 'Allô-Couscous.' While we wait for our guests, let us pray together, it is nearly time for the *maghrib* prayer. But I do not want this witch under my roof," I murmured into my mother's ear. "We are believers, my mother . . . "

"Fine, my son . . . "

While my mother was explaining to the woman that she had to be on her way, I pulled my brother to one side and began to question him about his life, and ask him if he liked my apartment. I told him I had bought a little house with a garden, and that I would gladly give it to him as a wedding present.

"Thank you," said my brother, sniffing.

"Why are you crying?" I said, annoyed.

"From the emotion, my brother . . . "

"Not everyone has the honor to host forty pilgrims under his roof," I said approvingly, just as the witch finally went out the door.

My mother and my future sister-in-law came and unrolled their prayer mats and we said the prayer. After that we sat in a semi-circle. While I was grinning from ear to ear, my mother, my brother, and my brother's fiancée, their mouths open wide, could not stop staring at my walls.

"It's a lovely green, isn't it?" I said.

"A very pretty color," said my mother, gasping.

"It's nothing to cry over," I said, somewhat severely.

Then to my brother: "Let us read, my brother. Like in the old days."

"Like in the old days," echoed my brother, just as my first guests arrived.

There were three or four of them, I can no longer recall exactly. What I do remember is that not one of them looked anything like a pilgrim.

"*As-Salamu Alaykum*," I greeted them, without hiding my dismay, looking up and down at their firemen's uniforms, their clean-shaven faces, their boots, their embarrassed air.

Placing his hand on my shoulder, my brother explained that they hadn't wanted to take the risk of going through Paris in their Afghan clothing, they would for sure have been collared as vulgar terrorists . . .

"That's true," agreed my mother.

"And anyway," added my brother, "the others, who couldn't find a way to hide, are waiting for us in the new house, next to the Jean-Pierre-Timbaud mosque. Let's have the dinner there, it will be more discreet."

"Indeed," acquiesced my mother.

"Not a problem," I said. "I'll call 'Allô-Couscous' and give them the change of address, and we'll head over there."

"We can do it when we get there," said my mother.

"Fine, my mother," I said, pleased that my efforts were at last being rewarded, and that my plan had worked: that renegade's scheming had been thwarted.

Your mother will never give up. She will always be faithful to her principles and her education. As will you. Grandson of the master.

It was then that I saw the sheet of paper folded in four that my brother was holding in his hand.

"What's this?" I asked, grabbing it from him.

"It's your notes," said my brother.

"Your concierge gave them to us," said my mother.

"Don't go near that woman, my mother. She is dangerous," I said, unfolding the paper.

It did not look like my handwriting, but the ideas were mine, without a doubt. *I change the décor in my apartment. I invite guests. Pilgrims. And I marry a woman carefully chosen by my mother. An Algerian younger than twenty-two years old. We will live in the house on rue Jean-Pierre-Timbaud. Two stories, a little garden. Mademoiselle Papinot, from the Sèvres Agency, knows all about it. But I'll keep my apartment. Any trips to Greenland or Venus are out of the question. The sultan of Saint-*

Germain will end his days in this building, on rue Saint-Placide.
Just like Huysmans.

"She stole this from me."

"Yes my son," said my mother, weeping incessantly.

"I don't see why you're crying," I said, losing my temper.

Remembering the pilgrims who were just outside the door, I lowered my voice almost to a whisper and said, "I know you refuse to talk about this, my mother. A Muslim does not attempt to damage his own life. That is true. But Driss was a believer, my mother, just like you and me. And it is because of that woman that on Friday June 23, 2006, your nephew went mad and put an end to his days, my mother. I found out about it by reading and re-reading that damned manuscript that I discovered in my apartment. But I told no one. And in any case, no one would have believed me, my mother," I sobbed. "Just as no one will believe that when it is all over, that stealer of lives will move on to something else."

"It's not all over, my son," said my mother as we were going down the stairs, escorted by our august guests, greeted by my neighbors.

So kind.

So discreet.

So well integrated.

In an entire year we never heard a thing.

No visitors. Never went out.

Thank you, thank you, said my mother.

In the beginning, everything was fine. He only went out to buy cigarettes. He had everything delivered from the super-market and the delis. Lots of food, as if he were having friends over. I took care of the housecleaning. He had piles of books, all over the apartment. Then he took the keys back from me and started calling, full of reproaches, saying he couldn't find this or that, some piece of clothing, or a file. And he would ask me if a woman had come by to drop off some keys, and here he was someone who never had any guests. He lived like a hermit. I thought he must be going through a serious depression, that he'd get over it eventually, but after his sister's visit his condition only got worse. My name is Lisa Martinez, but he had decided that my name was Loubna Minbar . . .

Thank you, thank you, said my mother, abruptly curtailing the concierge's susurrations.

Once we were in the car, I whispered to my brother: "I met Loubna Minbar the day I signed the lease to my apartment. I arranged to meet her at the Café de Flore. She came with one of her books so that I could recognize her. I wanted to talk about Driss. Wanted her to tell me you know what. But we talked about everything but Driss. And then she vanished. Well, pretended to vanish. In fact, I never stopped seeing her. Sometimes she was a brunette, sometimes a redhead. Even a dyed blonde. Or a student. I am sure she thinks she fooled me with her disguises, just as she must have fooled Driss."

"No doubt," said my brother.

"And the concierge . . . "

"Yes?"

"That is her, too, I'm absolutely convinced of it."

"Really?" said my brother.

"That Portuguese accent she served up to us earlier on, it's just another trick. For she is none other than Loubna Minbar. A thousand faces. A thousand voices."

"God hath given you one face, and you make yourselves another," declaimed my brother, placing his hand on mine.

"Is that in the Koran?" I said, startled.

"It could be. But it's about Ophelia, in *Hamlet*," said my brother just as the car, big as a truck, set off into the Paris night.

"You read Shakespeare?" I said, somewhat dazed.

"From time to time . . . "

"That's good, my brother . . . You should also read the Arab writers. Above all the poet-theologians. They know the art of combining mysticism with libertinage."

"Good," said my brother.

"But you must never open *The Sultan*. It's a collection of lies and insults with regard to those of us who have the faith, who have principles . . . You promise?"

"I promise."

"Excellent, my brother," I said, my mind suddenly caught up with thoughts of my little Versailles, my lovely divine nest that I would soon, very soon, after this simulacrum of a banquet, move back into. My nest, my marvel. Beautiful. White. Airy. Like a summer's breeze.

A moment later, I entered a world of fire and ice. Where wolves howl and men are silent.

A place where, he said to me, you have come to listen to me at last.

About the Author

Leïla Marouane was born in Tunis in 1960 and has lived and worked in Paris since 1990. In addition to *The Sexual Life of an Islamist in Paris*, she is the author of four novels and one collection of short stories. In 2004, she was awarded the Literatur Prize at the Frankfurt Book Fair, and in 2006 she was the recipient of the prestigious Prix Jean-Claude Izzo for her novel *La jeune fille et la mère*.